"GET THAT BLOUSE OFF, HERE AND NOW," FARGO ORDERED.

"You've got to wash off that perfume you're wearing—the Kiowa won't have any trouble picking up our scent. Now, do you want to do it yourself, or do I do it for you?"

"You wouldn't dare," Millicent snapped— regretting the words at once, as he smiled at her. "Of course you would. You'd enjoy it, wouldn't you?"

"I might. Never washed down an icicle before," Fargo said.

"Icicle!" she echoed, her brilliant blue eyes shooting blue flames.

Fargo pulled her into his arms. "One good thing about icicles . . . they melt," he drawled, then his mouth came down hard on hers. . . .

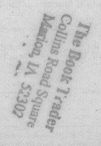

Exciting Westerns by Jon Sharpe

KIOWA KILL

by
Jon Sharpe

A SIGNET BOOK

NEW AMERICAN LIBRARY

NAL BOOKS ARE AVAILABLE AT QUANTITY DISCOUNTS
WHEN USED TO PROMOTE PRODUCTS OR SERVICES.
FOR INFORMATION PLEASE WRITE TO PREMIUM MARKETING DIVISION,
NEW AMERICAN LIBRARY, 1633 BROADWAY,
NEW YORK, NEW YORK 10019.

SIGNET TRADEMARK REG. U.S. PAT. OFF. AND FOREIGN COUNTRIES
REGISTERED TRADEMARK—MARCA REGISTRADA
HECHO EN CHICAGO, U.S.A.

SIGNET, SIGNET CLASSIC, MENTOR, PLUME, MERIDIAN AND NAL BOOKS
are published by New American Library,
1633 Broadway, New York, New York 10019

First Printing, November, 1984

1 2 3 4 5 6 7 8 9

PRINTED IN THE UNITED STATES OF AMERICA

The Trailsman

Beginnings . . . . they bend the tree and they mark the man. Skye Fargo was born when he was eighteen. Terror was his midwife, vengeance his first cry. Killing spawned Skye Fargo, ruthless, cold-blooded murder. Out of the acrid smoke of gunpowder still hanging in the air, he rose, cried out a promise never forgotten.

The Trailsman, they began to call him, all across the West: searcher, scout, hunter, the man who could see where others only looked, his skills for hire but not his soul, the man who lived each day to the fullest, yet trailed each tomorrow. Skye Fargo, the Trailsman, the seeker who could take the wildness of a land and the wanting of a woman and make them his own.

1861—Some called it the corner where the Utah and Wyoming territories touched. Those who knew called it Kiowa Country, and rode the land in fear . . .

1

Dammit to hell," the big black-haired man bit out angrily
s the pounding on the door continued. He swung his pow-
rfully muscled naked form from the bed as Sally Dix pulled
he towel up and her large, soft breasts disappeared. Or
lmost. It was a small towel, not really up to the task of cov-
ring Sally's ample bosom. "Who the hell is it?" Skye Fargo
arked at the closed door of the hotel room.

"U.S. Army, sir," the voice called from the other side of
he door.

Fargo's thick black brows lowered in a frown. "U.S.
rmy?" he echoed.

"Yes, sir," the voice answered. Fargo frowned at the
voman in the big brass bed and Sally Dix shrugged bare
houlders at him.

He drew the big Colt .45 from the gun belt hanging over
he brass bedpost. "Open the goddamn door," he rasped.
Ie had the hammer pulled back as the door opened and the
lue-uniformed figure stepped into the room. Fargo low-
red the Colt as he took in the smooth-cheeked face, not
nore than nineteen years on it, he guessed. The soldier's
yes went to the bed where Sally tried unsuccessfully for

9

modesty under the towel. Fargo saw the young soldier pull his eyes away from her with an effort.

"Corporal Dexter, sir," the soldier said, standing stiffly. "Sorry to interrupt."

"That makes two of us," Fargo growled.

"Three," Sally said with a little laugh.

The corporal kept his eyes rigidly fixed on the big man's muscled form. "Captain Rogers wants to see you right away, sir," he said.

"Who's Captain Rogers?" Fargo barked.

"Commanding officer, Troop B, U.S. Cavalry, sir," the corporal answered.

"Ten soldier boys, one barracks at the end of town," Fargo heard Sally put in.

"Well, Corporal, you tell the captain I'm busy," Fargo said as he returned the Colt to its holster. "And I expect to stay busy for some time."

"Begging your pardon, sir, but the captain said you should come right now," the corporal answered.

"The only place I'm going to come now is right here, sonny," Fargo growled, and heard Sally's giggle.

He saw the corporal swallow. "But Captain Rogers said—" the soldier began again as Fargo cut him off.

"Pack it in," Fargo snapped. "You are putting off my pleasurin', soldier, and that irritates me. You've two seconds to get out of here."

"Yes, sir," the corporal said as he bolted from the room with a last glance at the bed where Sally was already flinging the towel aside. Fargo kicked the door shut and sank back onto the bed, and Sally Dix's arms encircled his neck at once.

"Damn, how'd that Captain Rogers know I was here?" he muttered.

"You brought in the Browder caravan. The whole town

10

nows you're here, and there's but one hotel in Spineyleaf," ally said.

"Suppose so," Fargo muttered as he lowered his face into ally Dix's big pillowy breasts. He rubbed his face into their nveloping softness, then pulled back, let his eyes travel up nd down Sally's ample body. Always a large girl, Sally still ad the body of a beautiful peach, everything round and elicately pink, luscious and soft. Only now it was a peach in anger of becoming overripe. The muscle tone in her reasts had gone just enough to allow a hint of sagging. Her egs were a little heavier, and her belly a little rounder and eshier. The years had been kind but had still left their nark. Yet Sally Dix's direct, simple, honest enjoyment of he pleasures of the body remained the same as when she'd vorked in a dance hall instead of owning one.

"Fargo, make the years all go away," she murmured as he pressed herself into him. Her hands began to roam up nd down his body, halting only to dig into his buttocks and ull him closer. Sally had never been one for slow prelimi- aries, he remembered well as he moved into the soft ave- ue of her thighs. Her flesh closing around his waist was varm and he felt his organ seeking, pushing, probing, and nally finding her sweet warmth, her dark tenderness. He eard Sally's groan of pleasure and moved slowly back and rth, pushing down and upward, down and up as if in a low, horizontal dance.

"Oh, yes . . . oh, yes . . . so good . . . so good . . . aaah," Sally groaned, and Fargo saw her lips curl in a Cheshire-cat smile. Her familiar sounds came to him— eep little laughs, pleasure-filled sighs—as her hands con- inued to dig into him. "Ah, yes, ah . . . ah, good . . . ah, 'argo . . . Fargo, good, good . . . ah, yes," Sally Dix mur- ured. Her movements quickened, her torso pushed eeper and longer, like a giant wave taking on new strength s it nears shore. The warm pressure of her fleshy thighs pulled tight against him and she let out a roar of pure joy. "Oh, Jesus, great, oh, great, wheeee . . . oh, great," she half-screamed as she exploded with him, her arms, legs and pillowed breasts enveloping him. Her head nodded vigorously in rhythmn with her inner spasms of pleasure until finally she slowed and slid away from him, her hands moving along his ribs, her legs rubbing slowly against him until they slipped away.

He pulled back and saw Sally's broad face smiling up at him. "Just the way it always was, Fargo," she said, and sighed happily. She held him against her breasts with their firm, brownish nipples. "I thought I'd be rusty," she said. "Don't do it hardly anymore. I let the girls take care of that."

"Glad you made an exception in my case," Fargo said. She ran her hands through his black hair as her eyes traveled over his chiseled handsomeness and grew suddenly almost sad. "You . . . you're old wine, Fargo. Can't ever turn down old wine," Sally Dix murmured.

"I'm holding you to your promise . . . a week," he said.

"It'll go too fast," she answered, kissed him, and pulled away, swinging her legs over the side of the bed. She stood and reached for the lavender dress and pulled it on over her full bottom.

"What are you doing?" Fargo frowned.

"Got to go back to lock up the cash box. We put away the cash twice a night," Sally said.

"You never said anything about this. I figured you'd be staying the night," Fargo protested.

"For God's sake, I'll be back in an hour." Sally laughed as she buttoned up the dress. "You just wait there and think about it, and you'll be all ready to go when I get back."

"I don't have to think about it. I'm ready now," Fargo grumbled. "Hell, this isn't fair."

"I'll be back. You can wait an hour," she said as she pulled he door open and sailed from the room, still carrying her shoes in one hand. He heard her little laugh as the door closed; he lay back on the bed and wiped the frown from his face as he thought about Sally. Six years since he'd seen her and suddenly it was as if it were only a few weeks back. The flesh makes its own remembering. But Sally had made her own life here in Spineyleaf, he reflected, a grubworm of a own with little past and an uncertain future. Not that much more could be expected from a small town sitting in the middle of Kiowa country with the Wasatch Range behind it and the rolling prairie land in front. Bringing the Browder caravan out from Kansas had been an unexpectedly hard run, filled with flooding and detours, up through Medicine Bow to skirt the Colorado Rockies.

He'd earned his week of pleasuring and he lay back and counted off minutes until the hour was almost gone. The hungers of the flesh and the anticipation were a potent combination and he felt himself responding as he lay naked on the bed and the hour drew to an end. The knock on the door was soft, feminine, and right on schedule. "No need for you to knock, honey. I'm just waiting for you," he called out. His eyes were on the door as it opened and she stepped into the room. He glimpsed a high-buttoned tan blouse and very blue eyes turning into blue saucers, full red lips dropping open.

"*Heavens!*" he heard the young woman gasp as she stared at him, her very blue eyes focusing on his erect, almost waving maleness. "Oh, my God," she gasped as she spun and raced from the room.

"Damn!" Fargo bit out as he swung from the bed.

"Would you *please* put something on," he heard the voice call from outside the open door.

"Sorry," he said as he climbed into his shorts. "You just got the wrong room, honey," he said with a chuckle in his voice.

"You said you'd been waiting for me," the young woman called back.

"Expected some other gal," Fargo said, and stepped to the doorway.

The young woman turned, her very blue eyes brilliant but full of disapproval as she stared at him. "Can't you put trousers on?" She frowned.

"Not going anywhere I'll need them," Fargo said laconically as he let his glance take in a fairly tall, slender shape with breasts that pushed the high-buttoned tan blouse out in nicely rounded twin mounds. He saw a thin, straight nose, delicate nostrils; light-brown, almost blond hair pulled up in a bun atop her head; pencil-thin brows that arched over the brilliant blue eyes; full, red lips that had no business being held as primly as they were—a strikingly attractive face despite the austere, severe, disapproving cast to it. She leveled a schoolteacher stare at him.

"Whether you were expecting some other young lady or not, no gentleman would invite anyone in in that state," she said.

"I'm not interested in any lecturing," Fargo said, his voice hardening.

"Those who need it most usually aren't," she said, sniffing with disdain.

"I told you, you just got your little high-toned ass in the wrong room," Fargo said.

"Obviously," she snapped as she started to turn away. "I was looking for a Skye Fargo."

"What for?" he asked in surprise.

She paused, the blue eyes sheathed in icy condescension. "I hardly think that's any of your concern," she answered.

"Might be." He shrugged. "Seeing as how I'm Skye Fargo." He turned and stepped back into the room and sat down on the bed. He lifted one leg up, rested on his elbows. She appeared around the edge of the open door a

14

moment later, the brilliant blue eyes staring at him, moving across his muscular, powerful body.

"You're not," she breathed.

"Sorry, but that's me," he said. "Now who in hell are you, honey?" he asked.

Her head lifted and she answered with a cold regality that might have done justice to a princess. "Millicent Madison," she said. "I left a message with the desk clerk telling you I'd be coming by this evening."

"Never got it," Fargo said, and chuckled as he recalled his words at her knock. "Few crossed signals," he said. "But you found me. Now you tell me why?"

He saw her eyes sweep over him with disapproval again. "I'm not used to talking to gentlemen clad only in their shorts," she said.

"Too bad," he commented, and saw the brilliant blue eyes flare. "Talk."

"I've a job for you, something that needs immediate attention," she said.

"You and the U.S. Army," he grunted, and she frowned.

"I beg your pardon?" she said.

"That translates into no," Fargo growled.

"You haven't even heard me out," Millicent Madison said.

"Don't have to. Not interested. Come back in a week," he said.

"I don't have a week to waste," Millicent snapped.

"Me neither." He grinned as he stretched out on the bed. "Go find somebody else."

"You can't just turn me down like this," she protested, the brilliant blue eyes darkening.

"I just did, honey," he said.

"What do you have to do here for a week that's so important?" Millicent demanded.

"Screw, sleep, and eat, in that order," Fargo answered.

"You enjoy being crude?" she snapped.

"I enjoy being honest." He smiled.

"A life is at stake here," Millicent Madison said.

"Nothing new about that out here, honey," Fargo said.

"And you won't even hear me out?" she accused.

"I told you, come back in a week," Fargo said. "I've earned my pleasuring. I'm going to enjoy it."

"I can't wait a week, and you're a callous lout," Millicent shouted. She pulled the door open wider and stalked out of the room. "You're something, Fargo, really something," he heard her call back, and a half-second later he saw Sally's face appear, instant fury gathering in her eyes as she glanced back down the hall and then at him as he lay in his shorts across the bed.

"You bastard," Sally Dix hissed.

"Now, hold on, there," Fargo said as he swung from the bed, Millicent's heels still clicking down the hallway. "You've got it all wrong."

Sally's eyes held fury and he remembered the wildness of her temper. "You couldn't even wait an hour. You had to go get some chippie from the hotel," she said. "All that bullshit about waiting so long to see me again and I believed it."

"She just came to offer me a job," Fargo said.

"Offer you something, but it wasn't a job. I heard what she just said. You're something, Fargo, really something," Sally mimicked.

"She didn't mean what you're thinking. You've got it all wrong, dammit," he tried again, but saw rage still in Sally's eyes.

"You sure haven't changed any, I'll say that, except maybe for the worse," Sally blazed. "Your week just came to an end, you bastard."

"No, wait, listen to me. You've got it all wrong. Look, I'll go find her tomorrow. I'll get her to tell you herself," Fargo said.

16

"Meanwhile, you'll try to screw and sweet-talk me into forgetting and forgiving. You go to hell," Sally flung back. "You bring her to me tomorrow, let me hear her say it, and then we'll see. Till then, don't you come nosing around my place, you hear me?"

"Come on, wait," he tried, and reached for her arm. She pulled away from him and stalked into the hallway. "Goddamn, this ain't fair," he yelled.

"*Hah!* You're someone to talk about fair," she threw back as she strode away. She reached the stairway and he started to race after her and halted, realizing he was only in shorts. He turned back into the room to yank on trousers, gun belt, and boots. Seconds later he was racing down the hallway to take the stairs in three leaping strides. The lobby door was still swinging as he raced outside.

"Dammit, Sally, you hold that powder keg temper of yours," he shouted as he ran into the street. He skidded to a halt as the six uniformed figures blocked his way, each holding an army carbine. He saw the young, smooth-cheeked corporal at the end of the line.

"Captain Rogers' orders, sir," the corporal said. "He told us you weren't to leave the hotel except to go with us."

Fargo looked over the six soldiers, none much older than the corporal, he saw. Young faces, all distinctly uneasy. He cursed under his breath. He didn't want a shoot-out with the army, not without a hell of a lot better reason than this. "I just want to catch that gal that ran out of here," he said.

"Sorry, sir," the corporal said.

Fargo's eyes narrowed as he slowly scanned the line of troopers ending with the corporal. "Corporal Dexter, you know who you're playing games with?" he asked.

"Yes, sir, we've been told about you," the soldier said, and Fargo saw him swallow hard.

"Then you know I could take out at least four of you, maybe more, with my first volley," he said.

The corporal swallowed again. "Yes, sir," he said.

"And you're going to try and stop me," Fargo commented.

"Captain's orders, sir," the soldier answered. Fargo's grunt gave him credit for fighting down the fear that was so clear in his young face.

"You've more guts than brains, sonny," he muttered. "If that's the way it is, then I won't be leaving till morning."

"Whatever you say, sir," the soldier answered, but the relief was plain in his voice.

"Goddamn," Fargo muttered as he turned and strode back into the hotel; he almost tore the door from its hinges as he raged through it. The room shook when he reached it and slammed the door shut. There was a back stairway, but that still left Sally to argue with and he knew there'd be no convincing her this night. He turned the lamp out, flung clothes off, lay down on the bed, and cursed Sally and her damn temper. But Millicent Madison had been to blame for it, he bit out in silent anger. Her damn unexpected visit and her parting words. Signals crossed all over the place, he frowned.

He swore again and turned on his side, closing his eyes and letting sleep slowly creep over him. It was the only thing the night held for him, now. But, come morning, he'd find himself the high-nosed, lecturing little prude. She'd help him put his week back together or he'd have her ass for it.

2

The morning sun found its way through a lone, narrow window as Fargo woke and swung out of bed. He washed and dressed, using the big porcelain bowl and pitcher provided with cold water. His mood was still one of dark frustration and anger as he strapped on his gun belt and left the room. He went down the single flight of stairs to the seedy lobby with the elderly man behind the desk. "You had a goddamn message for me yesterday," Fargo barked. "You never gave it to me."

The man blinked through crinkled, watery eyes. "Sorry," he said. "Things sometimes slip my mind."

"Then get a broom and put somebody else behind the damn desk," Fargo snapped. "A gal left the message, Millicent Madison. She leave an address?"

"No, but she did say she was staying in town," the old man said.

Fargo turned the reply in his mind as he strode away. It had to mean she was at a private home somewhere, he muttered to himself. He pushed through the doorway and came to a halt outside as his gaze swept the six soldiers still there.

"Captain Rogers is still waiting, sir," the corporal said.

"I expected so," Fargo grunted. He walked to his horse at the hitching post and the Ovaro bobbed its head, the magnificent black forequarters and hindquarters glistening in the morning sun, the pure white midsection gleaming. He saw the corporal and the others mount their standard U.S. Cavalry bays as he swung onto the Ovaro. The corporal led the way as the other troopers pulled up in the rear, and Fargo rode silently except to swear to himself as he passed Sally's place. But she'd been right about the single barracks at the end of town, he saw as the corporal pulled up before the structure. It was actually a converted grain warehouse, Fargo noted. He halted the Ovaro in front of the doorway at the center of the building as an officer stepped outside. The captain's bars on his uniform gleamed brightly.

"Stay in the saddle," the captain said as he came forward.

Fargo saw a young man, perhaps thirty, of medium build with a trim body that he carried well. He had dark-brown hair cropped short above a face without a single distinctive feature except an air of barely suppressed bitterness that showed in the tightness of his mouth. "I'm Captain Rogers, Howard Rogers," the man said as he eyed Fargo astride the beautiful Ovaro. "You're a stubborn man, Fargo," the captain pronounced.

"That's been said," Fargo blandly agreed.

"You could've come last night after your lady friend walked out on you," Captain Rogers asserted.

"Didn't feel like it. Don't feel like it now. I'm just being accommodating. I've other things to take care of this morning," Fargo answered.

"No, I want you to come look at something with me," Captain Rogers said.

Fargo saw a trace of concern in the young officer's face and was curious. "Why me?" he asked.

"You're the one they call the Trailsman, aren't you? I'm told you're the very best tracker there is. I hear you know

he Indian like nobody else does," Captain Rogers said.
"You've a reputation, mister. When I heard you were here
n Spineyleaf, I figured to make use of you." Fargo said
nothing as he watched the captain swing onto a big bay with
a well-shined saddle. "Let's ride, I've had a burial party
waiting all night because of your screwing and
stubbornness."

"Things didn't go exactly as I wanted, either," Fargo said
coldly as he swung alongside the officer and the corporal.
The others fell in behind in a column of twos.

"I could've had you hauled in last night, you know," Captain Rogers muttered.

Fargo's smile was a striking contrast to the blue quartz of
his eyes. "You could've tried," he corrected. "But you know
what that would've meant and you don't have any troopers
to waste. So, Captain, let's cut out the big army-captain
bullshit. We'll get along better."

Captain Rogers held his hard stare for a long moment and
finally nodded curtly. "Guess so," the officer said, and set
off at a fast trot. He headed southwest toward the upper corner of the Utah Territory, and Fargo's eyes swept the terrain as a matter of habit.

"How come you have only ten troopers here?" he asked.

"I see you don't know Major Armsted," the captain said
with bitterness in his voice. "You know Fort Calder?" he
asked.

"North, some twenty-five miles," Fargo said. "Major
Armsted's the commander?"

"That's right, and the fort's more than a fort. It's his personal plum," the captain said. "Every wagon train heading
west over the Rockies or north into Montana stops there to
resupply. He's got a small village built into the fort. Major
Armsted's oasis, he calls it."

"You don't sound too happy about that," Fargo
commented.

21

The captain let a harsh sound escape his lips. "I'm not happy about being out here with ten troopers, most of 'em barely old enough to shave. What the hell good can we do anybody? We just about can protect ourselves, and that's a big maybe. Bill Schoonmaker feels the same way."

"Who's he?"

"Captain Schoonmaker. He's got ten troopers, too, up north at the edge of the Wind River Range. He's worse off than we are, with just two cabins in the middle of nowhere. We've got Spineyleaf here at least. Main thing is we're both hung out like sacrificial lambs."

"Want to nail that down better?" Fargo asked.

"In his reports to Washington, Armsted puts down that he's got patrols out, and that satisfies the brass. They don't know we're a joke, a token," the captain said.

"What's behind his doing this?" Fargo questioned.

"Armsted's making Fort Calder his own monument to himself. He doesn't care about anything else. He sits in his damn fort and he's safe. He sees to that by keeping every trooper he can right there."

"You're saying that's not right?"

"It's right to have a safe fort, but not at the expense of everything else. He could have a dozen properly manned patrols riding the territory. That'd do the settlers and wagon trains some good. Sitting like a toad on a rock doesn't help anybody except those who stop there for a few days. Before they get there and after they leave, they're on their own. The Indians have tried three attacks on Fort Calder, and failed each time. Armsted's going to make sure he stays safe there."

"While you're out here without enough strength or support," Fargo echoed.

"That's right, hung-out, sacrificial lambs," Captain Rogers said, the bitterness heavy in his voice now. "Truth is, Fargo, I think Armsted's afraid to take the field against

he Crow or the Kiowa or any of them. He's afraid he'd be
defeated. This way he has his cake and eats it. He's safe and
he comes off as being the big protector." The captain
increased his speed as he led the way down into a tree-
bordered hollow of land

Fargo spotted the three troopers standing guard at once,
and he saw them snap to attention. His nostrils flared as
they picked up the rancid odor. He reined to a stop alongside the captain. The odor was stronger and rottener.
Fargo's eyes moved across the hollow and the corners of his
mouth pulled down in distaste. He counted twelve
bodies—men, woman, children. All were stark-naked,
looking like so many broken dolls that had been stripped
and tossed aside, their arms and legs at grotesque angles.
Fargo dismounted and felt the captain's eyes on him as he
slowly walked among the naked bodies. He saw that the
attackers had enjoyed themselves with the women before
killing them. The children had simply had their heads
mashed in by club or tomahawk. He peered at the arrows
that protruded from some of the naked bodies, saw the col-
ors dyed onto the shafts near the feathers.

"Kiowa," he grunted. "When did you find them?"

"Last night, just before dusk," Captain Rogers said.

Fargo nodded, the answer explaining the odor that hadn't
had time to become sickening yet. The ground was chewed
up by the marks of horses and humans but he could see
enough to know that the Kiowa had had to number at least a
dozen bucks. He paused, his mouth a thin line, as he
peered down at two of the women. He'd seen too many like
it before, but he realized once again, there was no getting
used to it. He lifted his gaze to sweep the hollow of land
again. The captain's eyes were full of questions when Fargo
looked again at him.

"Go on, ask," Fargo said.

23

"Am I right in what I'm thinking? You've seen a lot mor
of these things than I have," Captain Rogers asked.

"You're right. I've never seen them stripped naked lik
these are," Fargo commented grimly.

"Thought maybe it was something I'd just never hear
about," the captain said.

"Indians will strip away whatever takes their fancy, mos
times guns, belts, necklaces, combs, knives, fancy buttons
sometimes boots," Fargo said. "But these are strippe
naked, every damn thing taken from them."

"We found three other wagons like this in the last fe
weeks," Captain Rogers said, and Fargo arched his brow.

"Strange . . . damn strange," he muttered.

"Got any ideas why?" the captain asked.

"Beats me," Fargo said, and cast a sideways glance at th
captain. "Anything else strike you as different?"

Captain Rogers frowned. "No, not that I can say," h
answered.

"Where are their wagons?" Fargo asked quietly, an
watched the captain's eyes grow wide as he glanced quickl
across the hollow.

"Jesus, no wagons," the captain breathed, shock in hi
voice. "I never noticed that. Jesus, I never noticed it."

"Don't beat yourself for it. Sometimes we miss the bi
things right in front of our noses," Fargo said. He let hi
eyes move across the hollow and the naked bodies. "Tw
wagons here, I'd guess," he said. "Indians usually bur
wagons. Sometimes they leave them, but usually they se
the torch to them. A gesture on their part. Taking them
another new one." He walked along the edge of the hollo
where the land grew wooded, mostly gambel oak and re
birch, and he halted to point to the wagon tracks that le
into the woods.

The captain nodded unhappily. Fargo walked back acros
the hollow and knelt beside the mutilated bodies of tw

24

women. He forced himself not to turn away as he peered at the necks and shoulders, caked with dried blood that had run down from their scalped heads. He reached out and ran one finger along the base of the neck of one woman and across the shoulder of the other. He slowly rose to his feet.

"Both had blond hair worn long," he remarked.

"Does that mean anything?" the captain asked.

"Not by itself. Indians take a shine to fancy scalps," Fargo replied.

"The only scalping at the others was a woman." The captain frowned as he thought back. "Can't remember about the wagons."

"I'll be getting back to town now," Fargo said as he walked to his horse.

"Wait a minute," Captain Rogers said quickly.

"You brought me out here to hear my thinking. You were right. It's something different, but I don't know anything more than that," Fargo said.

"It's got to mean something," the captain said.

"Likely," Fargo conceded. "Indians don't change their ways without a reason. But I can't tell you anything more than that."

"You could find out more," the captain said as Fargo pulled himself onto the Ovaro.

"I told you, I've got other things to do," Fargo said.

"I'll pay you double the usual army scout's pay," Captain Rogers said. "If something's in the wind, I need to know it. I need you to follow through and find out."

"Not interested," Fargo said. "Not for now, anyway."

"I don't want to wait. You know I have the authority to press any civilian into service if I need to," the captain said.

Fargo fastened him with a cold stare. "You're being dumb again, Captain," he said. "You know that won't work with me."

The captain's lips tightened unhappily. "Yes, I know it,"

he muttered. "But dammit, Fargo, I'm trying to do my job, which is protecting settlers and wagon trains, and I need help. Just give me something to go on. Let me know if this is just some crazy band of bucks or if it means something more. That's all I'm asking and I'll let the army pay well for it." He halted as he saw the big man studying his face. "What are you thinking?" he glowered

"I'm wondering whether you're dedicated or scared," Fargo said.

The captain reflected for a moment. "Both, dammit," he answered.

Fargo drew a deep sigh. The captain was honest and he liked that. Honest, uncertain, scared, and sure as hell in need of help. His thoughts broke off as a figure suddenly came into view, riding down along the top of the slope where the land was cleared in a patch some twenty-five yards wide. Bronzed, near-naked body gleaming in the sun, sitting on a pinto pony, the Indian raised his arm and shook the tomahawk in his fist as he raced his horse acros the clear land.

"Goddamn," Fargo heard Captain Rogers shout. "Let's get him." He saw the captain send his big bay into full pursuit and the six troopers race after him.

"Wait, dammit," Fargo called out, but the captain was racing on, charging up the slope after the bronzed figure his troopers close behind him. "Ah, shit," Fargo swore as he wheeled the Ovaro and sent the horse into the woodland veering sharply to the right. He pushed the horse into a gallop, bending in the saddle to avoid low branches as he rode parallel to the captain and the troopers. He heard the whooping cries before he glimpsed the six bucks as they raced into the open, between the lone Indian and the captain. Kiowas, Fargo grunted as he saw the design on the gauntlet one of the Indians wore on his wrist. They joined ranks with the first Indian who had come into sight and aced up the slope, making no attempt to circle and fight. Fargo swore again as the captain continued in headlong pursuit.

The Kiowa raced upward in a long curve, leading the troopers northeast. Fargo rode parallel, just inside the line of trees. It took perhaps two minutes more than he'd estimated, but suddenly the Kiowa parted, the six warriors separating in all directions. He saw the captain slow, taken by surprise and momentarily uncertain which one to pursue. The moment of indecision was all the Kiowa needed, of course, and they were all quickly out of reach. But Fargo's Ovaro hadn't broken stride for even a split second and he galloped on as one of the Kiowa raced into the trees almost directly in front of him. The Indian caught sight of him as he came up on his left and pulled his pony in a sharp turn to charge directly at the intruder.

Fargo kept the Colt in its holster. A dead Kiowa couldn't answer questions. Instead, he pulled the big Sharps rifle from its saddle case as the Kiowa raced at him, tomahawk in his right hand. He turned the rifle in his hands to hold it by the barrel. His eyes narrowed as he watched the Indian race toward him. The Kiowa, lips drawn back, leaned out of the saddle and raised his tomahawk. His black eyes glittered with hate, and Fargo took a new grip on the big Sharps as he saw the Indian swing the tomahawk in a flat, sideways arc. As the Kiowa's weapon curved through the air, Fargo dropped low, almost onto the Ovaro's withers, and felt the tomahawk brush through his black hair, sending his hat flying. Using the stock end of the rifle as a lance, he rammed it forward into the side of the Kiowa and felt at least one of the Indian's ribs snap.

The pony raced on, but Fargo heard the Indian grunt in pain as the blow sent him toppling from the smooth back of his mount. Fargo reined up and leapt to the ground, still clutching the rifle by the barrel. The Kiowa regained his feet but stayed half-bent over, one arm held to his broken rib and his flat, broad face grimmacing in pain. Fargo moved in and started to bring the rifle down on the Kiowa's head when the Indian hurtled his tomahawk. Already committed to the downward blow, Fargo could only twist to one side. He felt the tomahawk slam a glancing blow to his shoulder, that sent a spasm of pain down his arm. He stumbled sideways and the rifle dropped from his hands. He spun again, to see the Kiowa lunging at him, a hunting knife in his hand.

The Indian brought the hunting knife upward in a vicious arc. Fargo flung himself backward as he heard the blade whistle past his chest, a hairsbreadth away from ripping him open from belly to throat. He rolled and the Kiowa lunged forward again, this time thrusting the knifeblade out straight. Fargo only managed to get to one knee and bring an arm up before the Kiowa was on him. Using his weight and the Kiowa's momentum, Fargo lifted, kicked out, and sent the Indian sailing head over heels through the air in a backflip. He heard the Kiowa's half-scream of pain and leapt to his feet. The Indian half-rose, the hunting knife protruding from his abdomen. Only the hilt was showing. "Damn," Fargo swore as the Indian tried to pull the blade free, strength and life quickly deserting his bronzed body. The Kiowa fell forward and rolled onto his back. Fargo was at his side in one long stride. He dropped to one knee as the Indian stared up at him. Fargo knew enough of the Kiowa tongue to bite out the curt questions.

"Naked. Why?" he asked. "Wagons. Why?"

The Indian's almost lifeless eyes had enough hate in them to glitter for a last time. He moved his lips and bloody spittle dribbled from between them. The words followed on a last, gasped breath. "Tarawa . . . Thunder Chief . . . kill all," he said before his eyes closed for the last time over their hate.

"Damn," Fargo said again as he rose to his feet. He heard the sound of the hooves galloping into the trees. The Kiowa's final scream had carried to where Captain Rogers had halted, and Fargo saw the troops appear. The captain came to a halt and stared down at the Indian.

"Tried to take him so's he could talk. Didn't work out," Fargo said as he retrieved his hat and rifle.

"I wondered what happened to you," the captain said.

"What happened to me was I didn't rush off like a damn fool," Fargo said as he put the big Sharps into its saddle case. He speared the captain with a jaundiced glance. "You sure do need help because you don't know shit about Indians," he growled.

"I saw a chance to get one of them and took it." The captain frowned. "He didn't expect to see us."

"Hell, he rode out there just so's you'd go chasing after him like a hound after a bitch in heat," Fargo tossed back disgustedly. "The others came into it to make sure you'd keep on chasing after them. When they were ready, they took off and left you chasing the wind."

"Why?" the captain asked, and looked unhappy.

Fargo let his lips purse for a moment. "I'd guess to give the others chance to finish covering up the wagon tracks. They wouldn't have had a chance to do it right in the dark last night." He climbed onto the Ovaro and headed the horse down the slope and back toward the little hollow. "Let's go take a look," he muttered as the captain came up alongside him. "I got a name for you," he said. "Tarawa . . . Thunder Chief."

Captain Rogers looked anxiously at the big man beside him. "Tarawa . . . Thunder Chief," he echoed. "Mean anything to you?"

"Nope," Fargo said. He rode the rest of the way in silence, and when they reached the hollow, he guided the horse up the slope at the other side where the wagon tracks rolled into the trees. The tracks went on for a few hundred yards and then disappeared, all marks smoothed away. He watched as the captain stared at the ground.

"They use branches, pull them back and forth across the ground until there are no more tracks left," Fargo said. "Where there's heavy grass they'll sometimes use a travois and pull it in the opposite direction to stand the grass up again." He turned his horse back down the slope. The captain followed, his even-featured face clouded with dismay and discouragement. "I'll stay here and help with the burial work," the captain said. "We'll ride patrol when we've done with it." He paused, searched the big man's chiseled face. "Thanks for helping out back there," he said.

Fargo nodded and let his eyes sweep the hollow once more. "It does make me wonder, I'll admit," he said. "They're going to a damn lot of trouble. There's got to be a reason for it."

Eager hope leapt into the captain's face. "Then you'll try to find out? You'll scout for me?" he said.

"Not so fast," Fargo cut in. "I told you I've some things of my own to do first."

"Time may be important," the captain said.

"If they are up to something, they're not ready to move. They're still putting pieces together," Fargo said.

"Jesus, Fargo, I wouldn't know where to begin, and I don't have anybody else," the captain said.

"Maybe, when I'm finished with my own business," Fargo said. "I'll be in touch. Meanwhile, watch what you go chasing after."

"I'll remember that," Captain Rogers said, and the gratefulness in his voice was real.

Fargo turned and sent the Ovaro trotting up the slope that led out of the hollow. He rode slowly back toward Spineyleaf, the image of the naked, twisted, brutalized bodies clinging to his memory. But the sight of the victims of an

Indian attack always clung. It stayed inside a man like a sickening, sour taste in the mouth. Yet this one had been different and even the captain had recognized that much, for all his inexperience. At least his instincts had been right. Fargo felt himself feeling sorry for Captain Howard Rogers and his ten green troopers. The captain's description circled in his mind: sacrificial lambs. The words fit closely enough.

But hellfire, he didn't want to get involved with some crazy Kiowa chief who had his own twisted ideas of revenge. He wanted his week with Sally. He'd earned it, she'd promised it to him and that damn well came before anything else. Tail first, trail later, he muttered silently, and his lips drew tight. But first he had to set things right, and that meant finding a certain high-toned filly.

He quickened the Ovaro's trot and crested the top of a gentle rise to head down a path that took him alongside a pair of full-bottomed hackberries. He'd almost reached the trees when a figure sitting calmly astride a dark-gray gelding, moved out from behind the first hackberry. The frown dug deeper into his brow as he reined to a halt. She wore a yellow blouse, buttoned high to the neck again, and he knew he was unable to keep the surprise from his face. Her almost blond hair glowed in the sun and her brilliant blue eyes gazed at him with cool regality.

"I see you weren't being arrested," Millicent Madison said. "I watched the troopers ride off with you, and I followed for a while, wondering, I must confess."

"You wondered wrong," Fargo growled. "But you're here and that saves me looking for you."

"I decided to ignore your uncouth behavior last night and forgive your bad manners," Millicent Madison said with lofty condescension.

"Honey, I don't give a damn about your ignoring or forgiving. I care about your explaining," Fargo returned.

"Explaining? You mean, about why I want to hire you?" she said almost smugly.

"I mean about the gal you passed in the hall last night," Fargo said.

Millicent's condescension stayed. "Miss Dix? She runs the local dance hall, I'm told."

"She does, and she thinks I got it on with you last night while I was waiting for her to come back," Fargo said.

Millicent Madison's frown was instant, shocked disbelief seizing her face. "No," she gasped. "She couldn't possibly think such a thing."

"She could, and she did. She took that last thing you tossed back at me the wrong way," Fargo told her.

"The fruits of a dirty mind. Or perhaps she just knows you too well," Millicent said disapprovingly.

"Whatever, but you're going to straighten it out, Millie," Fargo said.

"*Millicent!*" she snapped back. "Millicent, not Millie."

"Whatever you like, Millicent, honey, but you're going to explain last night to Sally Dix," Fargo said.

Millicent's delicate nostrils flared. "I'll do no such thing. I'm not going to explain my actions to some dance-hall madam of yours," she returned.

Fargo felt his irritation harden at her icy condescension. "Hell, you won't," he rasped. "I was promised a week of fun and you loused it up for me last night. Now, you're going to set it right if I have to haul your high-toned ass there myself."

He saw the moment of uneasiness that flooded into the brilliant blue eyes, but she swept it away with instant bravado. "You can't force me to say something I don't want to say," she threw back.

"I can try," Fargo said blandly, and waited as she studied him, her eyes narrowing. He could almost see the thoughts racing behind those brilliant blue eyes. Even the conde-

cending iciness didn't dissipate her striking attractiveness,
e noted.

"I'll tell you what. I'll do it for you if you agree to help
ne," Millicent Madison offered.

"No deal, honey," Fargo snapped. "I don't even know
vhat you want and why."

"You wouldn't even hear me out last night," she threw
back rightfully.

He let his lips purse for a moment. "I'll do this for you.
ou square things with Sally Dix and I'll listen to you," he
aid.

"I square things and you're free to enjoy your week of
un," she said icily.

"That's none of your concern, honey. I'll hear you out.
hat's what you want, isn't it?" he countered.

"I want more than that," Millicent sniffed.

"Can't get more till I hear what you want," Fargo said
damantly. He watched her consider his offer, and her
mile was totally unexpected, a sudden burst of warmth.

"All right," she agreed, a note of smugness in her voice
hat made him frown inside. "You've a deal. I'll explain last
ight to Miss Dix. But alone, thank you. It'll be embarrass-
ng enough."

Fargo felt irritation stab at him. "Will it, now? I can think
f a lot of gals who'd not be at all embarrassed if somebody
hought they'd gone to bed with me. Fact is, they'd be right
lattered."

"I'm sure you can," Millicent said archly. "I'm sure you
ppeal to many women, those who like a kind of animal
ensuality."

Fargo grinned at her. "Why, that sounds like a compli-
nent, Millie," he said.

"Millicent," she snapped. "And I hardly meant it as that."

"Maybe you don't know what you mean," he remarked.
Or anything else much about yourself."

33

Her full, red lips tightened instantly. "I know all I need to know about myself, thank you," she sniffed.

He shrugged and ignored her glare. "When are you going to see Sally?" he asked

"Today, later on," she said. "But I'll expect you to hear me out before you start taking up with her again."

"That's the deal," he agreed. "Where?"

"Reverend Dobson's house, at the north edge of town," Millicent said. "A small, white house. Six o'clock."

He nodded and she started to turn the dark-gray gelding. "One thing now," he said. "How'd you come looking for me?"

"I asked about getting the best trailsman there is and was told that was you," she said. "Then I learned you were bringing the Browder caravan to Spineyleaf, a stroke of absolute luck." Her smile came again, not unlike an unexpected flash of sunlight. "Almost fate," she added. "I'll expect you at six."

He watched her ride away. She sat ramrod straight in the saddle but that didn't stop her breasts from bouncing beautifully together. He watched her go down the slope for a few moments longer, and then he turned the Ovaro under the trees. Millicent Madison was not just a prim little package. There was steel behind that proper primness, just as there were delicious curves behind her stiff, held-in airs. Something out of the ordinary was digging at her. He sensed dedication and principles as well as prudishness, along with whatever else had brought her here.

He slid from the Ovaro, unsaddled the horse, and sat down against the thick, gray-brown bark of a hackberry while the Ovaro grazed on gramagrass and sweet clover. Millicent Madison still circled in his thoughts. She'd taken his consent to hear her out as tantamount to agreeing to help her. He'd seen it in the way she had studied him before agreeing to talk to Sally. It was her condescending

34

arrogance that made her think that way. She'd learn better, he grunted. He'd made only one promise, and that was to Captain Rogers. But Millicent had made him curious, he admitted. But being curious didn't stand up to being horny, and he let himself think about Sally. She'd be contrite and apologetic and, he smiled, anxious as hell to make up for having misjudged him. Maybe, in a reverse kind of way, Millicent had done him a favor. He chuckled and turned off his idle thoughts to let his eyes move slowly across the rolling, tree-covered hills.

So rich, so beautiful, he murmured, and so deceptive, a land that seemed so quietly peaceful as it actually seethed with danger and death. Perhaps now more than ever, he frowned. Something strange was going on. The red man's rage was always there, but the Kiowa were giving it a new face. Tarawa . . . Thunder Chief. The name echoed in his mind. A chief striking out in his own ways? Or something more? Fargo again remembered the dead, naked bodies as he lay frowning against the tree. A gesture of rage? A kind of statement, reducing even the dead whites to a degradation beyond death and scalping? Fargo shook his head impatiently at the thought—that was white man's thinking. The Kiowa wouldn't see stripping their victims naked as any kind of degradation. But it had to mean something. It just didn't fit the pattern.

He broke off his thoughts as he saw the day begin to slide over the horizon. He rose, brushed the Ovaro before saddling up, and finally headed toward Spineyleaf as dusk fell. It was dark when he reached the town. He rode past the dance hall, which was just beginning to come alive for the night. He found the house easily enough. Millicent opened the front door as he dismounted. She'd changed from the yellow blouse into a form-fitting full-length dress that managed to be proper as it clung to her body.

"Please come in," she said.

He pulled his eyes away from her breasts, which pushed hard against the light-blue dress. He stepped into a sparsely furnished living room, almost austere, with but a half-dozen high-backed chairs and a plain pine cabinet in one corner. The walls were bare except for a wooden cross hanging on one side. Millicent was quick and sharp, Fargo saw, catching his reaction to the room at once.

"Reverend Dobson is a severe man. He doesn't believe in frills of any kind. He's a Methodist missionary," she said.

"Where is he?" Fargo questioned.

"In China. He gave me permission to use his home here," Millicent answered. "He's also my uncle."

"You some kind of missionary, too?" Fargo asked.

"No. I'm a teacher. That's how I became involved in this terrible thing," Millicent said. "But first, I want you to meet someone."

She turned and hurried into an adjoining room. When she didn't consciously hold herself in primly, her hips moved with a sinuous rhythm, Fargo noted. She returned leading a small, slightly built, balding Chinese gentleman, who was no taller than her shoulder. His skin seemed to be made of fine tracings, and he had a long, thin growth of hair under his chin, something betweeen a goatee and a beard.

"This is Mr. Soong," Millicent said. The little man bowed and immediately perched on the edge of one of the high-backed chairs. "Mr. Soong is one of the wealthiest merchants in China," Millicent said. "He hired me three years ago to teach his daughter, Mai-lin. I was hired because I knew Chinese. My uncle taught me the language. My position in the Soong household was to teach Mai-lin English and to generally educate her in Occidental culture. Of course, she had many other teachers. A wealthy Chinese girl is taught many things as part of her education."

"I've heard that. Not all of it book-learning, I'm told." Fargo smiled.

Millicent ignored his remark, but a moment of disapproval in her eyes told him she had understood it completely. "Mr. Soong planned for the time Mai-lin would help him in his extensive trade with British and American merchants," she went on.

"This is all very nice, but how does it send you looking for me?" Fargo cut in with some annoyance. He felt his brows lift in surprise as the elderly Chinese gentleman answered.

"My daughter has been abducted," the little man said, his English not so much accented as overly precise. "She was taken by slave traders."

"Slave traders?" Fargo echoed.

"Perhaps you are unaware of the size of the slave trade out of the Orient," Millicent said.

"I've heard tell of it," Fargo said.

Mr. Soong spoke again, his face impassive as he spoke, only the flicker of his almond-shaped eyes revealing any emotion. "Girls are seized and taken all over the world to be sold, usually into prostitution, sometimes as personal playthings for wealthy men," he said. "The trade with the Yankee slave traders has increased since you have established relations with China. But my own people share the blame, the warlords and the unscrupulous money-mad men. They seize the girls and sell them to the slave-trade captains. Evil always finds evil." He paused and seemed lost in thought for a moment. "Usually the traders do not have the chance to seize a girl of high breeding and culture such as Mai-lin. She was on a shopping trip when she was taken along with another girl. Millicent is here to find my daughter. Everything is in her hands. I have come to furnish only whatever funds she must have."

"You've got to have some reason to come out here looking for me," Fargo said, his eyes going to Millicent.

"We have learned that one of the outlets for the slave traders is someplace near here," she answered. "The girls

are taken by ship from China to California. Those who wi
fetch the highest prices are brought here by wagon. Som
never make it, of course, but enough do. We understan
buyers from all parts of the States come here for speci
girls. Mai-lin will be one of them."

"How'd you learn all this?" Fargo questioned.

Mr. Soong answered again, and Fargo caught the col
message behind the quiet words. "Some of my peopl
caught one of the slave traders, a small fish, but they con
vinced him to tell us what he knew."

"I have more details, but they can wait," Millicent cut in
"First, I need someone who can help find Mai-lin, someon
who can read signs, trails, and knows the ways of this savag
land. In short, you, Fargo. I've come as far as I can alone
Now I need you. Two thousand dollars in gold to find an
save Mai-lin."

Fargo felt the little whistle escape his lips. "A lot
money," he murmured.

"Indeed," Millicent said.

"I'll think on it," he said.

Millicent's little smile held that note of cool confidenc
that rankled. "I'm sure you'll think the right way. Whe
shall I expect you?" she answered.

"When you see me," he growled, and waited for he
instant annoyance. Instead, he received only another warr
smile.

"I'll expect that will be soon," Millicent said calmly. "I'
an incorrigible optimist."

He peered hard at her little smile, undaunted by h
frown, and he moved the Ovaro into the darkness. He rod
slowly through town, the meeting circling in his thought
The money offered wasn't the kind a man just turned awa
from, he mused. But then he'd turned down good mone
before. Besides, he half-smiled, there was no reason why h
couldn't have his cake and eat it. Millicent Madison neede

im. She'd wait a week. She'd be furious every minute of it, but she'd wait. There wasn't a hell of a lot else she could do, he reflected, not without a certain satisfaction. She was so goddamn sure of herself. A little taking down would do her good.

He halted outside of the dance hall and pushed away further thoughts of the meeting with Millicent and Mr. Soong. He dismounted, tethered the Ovaro to the hitching post, and made his way into the dance hall. The brightness and noise was almost a physical blow. He stopped and looked across the smoky room, the tinny piano hardly audible over the noise. A half-dozen cowhands spun four girls around the dance floor, no two of them keeping the same step or rhythm. He finally found Sally; she was at the end of the room helping to dispense oversize pitchers of beer. A curtained doorway hung behind her, and he made his way across the room, edging by the card players at the tables.

She didn't see him until, as he reached her, she turned, a huge pitcher of beer in one hand. Her frown was instant. Her hand closed tightly around the pitcher of beer and her eyes darkened. "You've got some nerve coming in here," she hissed.

Fargo felt the frown pull his brows together. "What do you mean? Didn't she come talk to you?" he asked.

"Oh, she was here all right and she told me the truth," Sally said scathingly. "She said she felt sorry for me."

"What the hell are you talking about?" Fargo growled as he felt a stab of uneasiness in his stomach.

"She told me how you paid her to come say she didn't go with you last night, but she decided not to lie to me," Sally flung at him. "She told me how you went looking for a woman last night, found her, and took her to bed."

"The bitch. The little bitch," Fargo swore through lips that hardly moved.

"Don't you call her names for telling the truth, Skye

39

Fargo," Sally flared. "I give her credit for it." Sally's arm
came up and Fargo saw the pitcher of beer lift with it. He
started to twist away, but the beer sailed through the air and
hit him full in the face. "That's for you, Skye Fargo. Don
you ever come 'round here again."

He shook the beer out of his eyes in time to see Sally dis
appearing through the curtained doorway. "You wait
goddammit," he shouted. He barreled through the curtai
to see a door slam shut in a little corridor. He curled his bi
hand around the doorknob and gave it a yank. It was locked
"You open up," he yelled, but there was no answer. "Wi
you listen to me, dammit?" he shouted as he rattled th
door.

Her voice came through the locked door, muffled bu
clear. "I can't hear you and I don't want to hear you," Sall
said. "I've got a shotgun pointed at that door and I'm goin
to shoot in three seconds if you don't get out of here, yo
lying bastard."

Fargo swore under his breath and stepped away from th
door. Sally wasn't the kind to bluff. There'd be no getting
her, even without a locked door between them. He kne
her temper. It'd take weeks for her to cool down enough
even listen to him. "Goddamn," he muttered as he turne
and pushed his way through the curtained doorway. H
wiped the residue of beer from his face as he strode throug
the dance hall. "That bitch," he cursed, and he wasn
thinking of Sally. "That stinking little bitch." All the triun
phant smugness suddenly explainted itself. He hurried ou
side and swung onto the Ovaro. His anger spiraled as h
sent the horse galloping across town to rein up before th
small white house.

A light burned in the living room as he leapt to th
ground. He was striding toward the door when it opene
and Millicent stepped outside, the light behind he

40

utlining the willowy curves of her body. "You little bitch," he roared.

Millicent's cool loveliness stayed infuriatingly composed, er thin brows arching disdainfully. "I expected you'd be omething less than a gentleman about it," she sniffed.

"Good. Then you won't be surprised that I'm going to fan our high-toned little ass," he said.

He caught fright glimmer for an instant in the brilliant lue eyes, but she kept her clool, he saw with reluctant dmiration. "That won't change anything," she countered.

"It'll make me feel better," he threw back.

"Brute strength is the resort of those without the mind or he wit to think of anything else," she snapped.

"Don't give me any more of your schoolmarm lectures," argo returned. "Christ, you've got nerve, lecturin' and yin' at the same time."

"Important things sometimes make little lies necessary. esides, you brought it on yourself," she said

"What?" He frowned

"That's right," she answered righteously. "All you anted was me to give you your week of fun back. You adn't any intention of cutting even a day off or even nswering me till then." He frowned back, unable to deny he truth she stabbed at him. "So now you've no reason to aste a week. You can start at once."

"Forget it," he bit out.

"Two thousand in gold, Fargo," Millicent said, and aned against the edge of the doorway. The light from nside curled around the full curves of her breasts as they ose above the thin line of her waist. The fine delicacy of her ace approached real beauty. "Sleep on it. You'll feel differnt, come morning," she said. "I don't see you as the kind of an to turn down good money just because you've been utmaneuvered."

He heard the laughter in her voice as she enjoyed what

41

she plainly saw as her victory. She was right enough, he conceded silently and angrily. He'd not be spending a week of fun with Sally. But she'd pay for that victory, he promised himself. He wasn't sure just how and when, but she'd pay for it. He'd be damned if he'd let a lecturing little filly pull this off. As he turned and climbed onto the Ovaro, his eyes were the blue of an ice-bound lake.

"Good night, Fargo. I'll expect you in the morning," she called as he slowly turned the horse away. He rode into the dark, not looking back as angry thoughts continued to simmer through him. Millicent Madison was lovely enough and desirable enough to make pay and she was confident she had him pegged. He'd do nothing to change that little piece of arrogance, now. But he'd find a way to make it backfire. He quickened the pinto's pace as he reached the end of town and rode into the low hills. He found a good spot under the wide branches of a red oak and he bedded down for the night.

3

The morning sun was warm as he woke, but he still felt angry as he washed and dressed. He got his gear together and rode from beneath the big oak. He steered the Ovaro up into the hills and he let his thoughts drift. He rode slowly, casually, until he halted on the side of a gentle slope to peer north where the land grew flat and then hilly against the horizon. Fort Calder lay on the other side of those hills, which reminded him that he'd promised to pay Captain Rogers a visit. Fargo slowly viewed the nearby hills and suddenly frowned, peering harder, every muscle tensed at once.

Something had moved on the next hill in the tree-covered slope, and he strained his eyes to see. It moved again—trees shook and then a flash of ponies moved downhill. He glimpsed at least two and was certain there were more, riding hard. "Damn," he swore as he sent the Ovaro lunging forward. The Indians were riding with speed and purpose, and that meant only one thing: they were on the chase. He stayed inside tree cover as he sent the Ovaro down to the bottom of the slope and up the next hill. He glimpsed the Indian ponies again, a brief flash of near-naked riders before they disappeared down the other side of the hill. He flung curses into the wind as he raced the Ovaro through the trees and crested the top of the second hill. The Ovaro was devouring distance and time as he started down the other side, but the Indians had too much of a head start. He rode recklessly through narrow spaces between thin white birches to try to make up time. The Ovaro half skidded on a patch of wet lichen, but regained his balance. Fargo slowed enough to head down the slope as it grew steeper.

He heard the sound of war whoops and cursed again as he raced downward. The trees grew thick and suddenly four horsemen appeared, racing up toward him. They slowed in surprise when they saw him. One carried a sack with part of a dress streaming from it. The two beside him carried only their bows, but the fourth held two small, reddish scalps hanging from a rawhide thong around his waist.

"Son of a bitch," Fargo bit out as he drew his Colt and fired in one swift motion. The Indian with the scalps flew from the back of his pony as though yanked by invisible wires as two of the Colt's heavy slugs slammed into him.

Fargo didn't wait to watch as he vaulted from the Ovaro, but he heard the whistling sound of the three arrows that split the air over the saddle. He hit the ground with both feet, slid, fell, and then rolled into a thicket of brush. He spun up onto one knee, the Colt raised to fire. He had expected to see the three Indians charging at him on their ponies, but he saw only one of the remaining three, leaning far out of his saddle to scoop up the two scalps from the one he had blasted away. Fargo fired another pair of shots, but the Indian stayed flat atop his pony, almost hanging from one side. The two shots just grazed their mark as the pony raced into the trees. Fargo rose to a crouch and looked around, the Colt ready to fire again. The three Indians were

:ing up the slope. He felt the ground tremble with the
pact of their ponies' galloping feet.

Fargo straightened, his mouth a thin, angry slash across
s face. They hadn't wanted to fight, even though they out-
mbered him. Getting away with the scalps and whatever
se they'd taken had been all important. They were plainly
der orders to hit and run. He frowned as he walked to
ere the dead Indian lay spread-eagled on the ground, his
e full of fury even in death. Fargo's glance paused at the
d man's moccasins. "Kiowa," he spit out aloud as he
ned away and whistled softly. The Ovaro appeared and
tted over to him. He mounted and rode the horse down
e slope to the bottom where it leveled, knowing what he'd
d and hoping against hope that he'd be wrong. You
ays hoped, but you were almost always wrong.

He swore again as the lone wagon came into view. He
ned the pinto to a halt and stared down at the four bod-
, each stripped naked: a man, a woman, and two chil-
en, both girls. Only the children had been scalped, he
ted grimly. He moved the Ovaro in a circle around the
ge of the scene and found nothing else unusual. He
sed those with the blind faith to come into this land with
t a single wagon, these children of hope . . . or
lousness.

He steered the horse away and headed for town. He'd
y that visit to Captain Rogers and let him send out a burial
ail. Thoughts rolled through his mind like tumbleweed
he rode. The Kiowa were up to something. This Tarawa,
under Chief, had a special plan. These raids, this brutal-
, had no randomness about them. But why? The question
ng in front of him. Rogers and his pitiful platoon would
ver find the answer, but somebody had better before it
s too late. Fargo made a distasteful face. Working for
ny pay didn't appeal, but that thought brought Milli-
t's offer rushing through his mind. That money was

45

worth the effort. They both needed him and together they
make the money part of it worthwhile. His thoughts beg
to take shape, almost enough to make him smile. He h
concern for Rogers, sympathy for Mai-lin, and a score
settle with Millicent Madison. Maybe he could roll them
into one package.

The thought intrigued him. He had a plan by the time
reached the lone barracks building at the end of town.
might have smiled but for the memory of the slain, nake
bodies that clung in his mind. He halted, took in the line
cavalry horses tethered to one side, and swung to th
ground. A trooper stood beside the doorway to the lo
building, but made no move to question him as he entere
He stepped into a room with a desk, a territory map, and
coat hanger. Two highbacked chairs completed the furnis
ings. Captain Rogers looked up from behind the desk
stare at him with a mixture of apprehension and hope.

"First things first. Send out a burial detail," Fargo sa
with grim flatness.

"Ah, Jesus," the captain said, angry sorrow flooding
voice instantly. "Where?"

"Bottom of the first set of hills heading north," Far
answered as he eased his big frame into one of the chai
The captain barked orders to the trooper at the door a
returned his gaze to the big man in front of him. "Sa
thing, with one change. Only the two kids scalped," Far
said, and watched Captain Rogers press his hands to his fa
for a moment.

"Christ," the officer said at the end of a long groan. "W
the hell does it mean?"

Fargo shrugged. "Something damn funny's going on,"
said. "I'll scout for you."

The captain studied him for a long moment. "Come
with any ideas?" he questioned, and Fargo shook his he
The captain reached into a drawer of the desk and pull

t a small roll of bills. He pushed it across the desk top at
rgo. "Scout's pay up front," he said. "But you're not
ing it for that. What made you decide?"

"Got a bad feeling," Fargo said. "Some kind of hell's
ing to break loose. I don't like to stand by and watch."

"Where the hell do you start?" the captain asked. "Try
d follow a trail?"

"Maybe. But first I go see an old friend, part fox and part
rd dog. He'll help me," Fargo answered.

"When do I hear from you?" the captain asked as Fargo
t the bills into his pocket and pushed himself out of the
air.

"When I've something to say," he answered.

He walked from the office without another word and
mbed onto the Ovaro. Millicent Madison was next, he
unted silently as he rode through Spineyleaf until he
ached the modest white house. The dark-gray gelding
s tethered outside, he noted. He dismounted and saw the
nt door open. Millicent stepped out, the yellow blouse
ll buttoned high and still pressing beautifully against the
rve of her breasts. She tried to read the chiseled impas-
eness of his face and finally gave up. But she made no
ort to keep the triumph out of the slow smile she offered.

"I really expected you sooner," she said.

"Had things to do," he told her. "Afraid you made a
stake?"

"Not really," she said. "I expected you wouldn't let pride
nd in the way of good money. I told you that."

"So you did," Fargo said. He saw the frown come into her
es at once as she studied him.

"Certainly you didn't decide to help me out of a sense of
inciple," she sniffed sarcastically.

"Nope," he answered. "Pay, one kind or another."

"What does that mean?" Millicent asked, her frown
epening.

"Whatever you want to make of it," he said. "I'm her
that's all you've got to know for now. Except one thi
more. I agreed to scout some for the army. The Kiowa a
up to something."

"Oh, no," Millicent said quickly. "I'm paying for yo
undivided efforts."

"It won't hurt you any, sort of one hand washing t
other. If I don't find out what the Kiowas are up to, your l
tle Mai-lin might never make it this far," Fargo said.

Millicent's loveliness remained severe as she frown
into space. "No, I want your full attention on finding M
lin," she decided.

He touched the brim of his hat as he turned to the Ovar
"Good luck, honey," he said.

"Wait," she called instantly, and he halted, his ey
uncompromising as he stared back. "Dammit, this is
fair," she protested.

"Fair's one thing. Right's another," he growled.

"All right," she muttered with her lovely, ruby li
pulled into a thin line. "But I don't like it."

"I'm all upset about that," Fargo said. "You said you h
more details."

"A name, somebody in Spineyleaf who acts as a cont
man," Millicent said. "We were told the slave traders co
tact him when a new lot of girls are coming in. His nam
Willie Rank."

"You try finding him?" Fargo questioned.

"No, I didn't know how I could without making som
body suspicious," Millicent replied.

"Showed some horse sense there," Fargo comment
"Anything else?"

"Only that Mai-lin has a special guard, a huge brute.
Mongolian Tartar named Kwang," she said. Fargo nodd
and started to swing up into the saddle. "The man Wil

seems the logical place to start," Millicent said. "You could set up a watch on him."

"Maybe," Fargo grunted. "Part of the time, anyway. It's hard to watch a man twenty-four hours a day. "

"We could take turns," she said

"Maybe," he said again. "There are other trails to check out."

"Such as?" She frowned.

"A thrush only needs a nest of twigs. A grizzly needs a cave," Fargo said, and Millicent's frown deepened. "Everything needs its own kind of place. The kind of operation you're talking about needs space as well as money, someplace to keep and hide the girls till the buyers come." He mounted the Ovaro.

"Where are you going?" Millicent asked.

"Visiting," he said. "An old friend who can help." He turned the horse around and saw Millicent start to climb onto the gray gelding. "I don't remember inviting you, honey," he growled.

"I don't need inviting," she said.

"No need for you," he said.

"You're making a contact. I want to be part of it. If something should happen to you, I want to be able to carry on," she said almost loftily.

"Something happens to me, honey, and there's not much you'll be carrying on," Fargo muttered.

"I'll save Mai-lin, somehow," she said, and the brilliant blue eyes flashed determination

"Or get yourself killed trying?" he stabbed back.

"That won't happen," she said, shaking away the remark.

He studied her determined face for a moment. "All right, come on. It might be good for you," he said.

"Why?" she asked.

"Teach you the difference between courage and stupidity," he said.

49

"You think it's stupid coming here to save a young girl from slavery?" Millicent shot back.

"Close to it. You and the old man come all the way out here with one name and a general idea of a place. Suppose you didn't make contact with me. What were you going to do, then?" he questioned.

"Try to find somebody else," Millicent snapped.

"And maybe find yourself nothing but trouble," Fargo said. "You want to come riding now with me. What happens to Mr. Soong? He just waits?"

"Exactly. The house is stocked with food. He's perfectly safe. We came in by night. No one knows he's there," Millicent said.

"You better hope it stays that way," Fargo grunted. "He'd be damn easy pickings. What if your one lead blows away and I can't pick up anything else?"

He saw the moment of despair pass through her face. "I don't know. I haven't thought it out that far. I came to save Mai-lin. That's all I really thought about. Dammit, is that so terrible?" she almost shouted, and he saw her blue eyes cloud as she looked quickly away.

"That's nice to see," he remarked. "You can really care."

She turned her glance back to him, in control again. "The idea of any young girl being kidnapped and forced into slavery disgusts me. Of course, I'm especially involved with Mai-lin after three years of being her personal tutor."

Millicent swung the gray gelding alongside him as they rode toward the rolling hills. A warm wind puffed at him and his nostrils flared as he caught the scent she was wearing—fresh, appealing and strong, with a touch of lilac in it. He glanced at her. "Very attractive," he grunted. "Your perfume."

"Thank you. Cologne," she said. "From France."

"You can wash it off at the first stream we reach," he said.

"Wash it off? You just said you liked it." She frowned.

"The Kiowa will like it, too," Fargo grunted.

"If they're this close to me, it won't make any difference," she said.

Fargo let a rush of air blow from his lips and controlled his temper. "They won't have to be this close to pick it up, honey," he said. "And I don't figure to debate this or anything else with you."

"I don't take ridiculous orders," Millicent snapped.

"You'll get used to it," he growled as he sent the Ovaro into a canter and headed up a timbered slope, mostly hackberry and white birch. She caught up in moments, just as he reined up beside a stream that coursed its way downhill. He looked past the trees to the next hills and the tree-covered ridgelines. His pursed lips as he looked back to the stream. It ran fast enough and deep enough, and he swung from the Ovaro. "Here and now," he said. "Get that blouse off and wash that stuff away."

"This is ridiculous." Millicent glared down at him.

"You want to do it yourself or do I do it for you?" he inquired politely.

"You wouldn't dare," she snapped, and her eyes retracted the words at once as he smiled at her. "Yes, you would, you'd enjoy it, wouldn't you?" she tossed at him.

"I might. Never washed down an icicle before," Fargo said blandly.

"Icicle," she echoed, the brilliant blue eyes shooting blue flame. "Better an icicle than a lot of things I could think of."

"One good thing about icicles," Fargo drawled. "They melt."

The blue eyes flashed again. "Not this icicle," she snapped.

"You have half a minute to get yourself in that stream," Fargo said, his voice suddenly harsh.

"And you're going to stand there and watch?" she returned.

"Wasn't planning to, but if that's what you want." He grinned.

"No, dammit, that's not what I want," she exploded.

He laughed as he wheeled the pinto away. "You sure about that?" he called back as he rode into the trees and dismounted. He climbed onto the lower branches of a thick hackberry and looked up to the top of the hill as he heard the sound of Millicent splashing in the stream. His jaw grew tight as he saw trees move, their branches bending and dipping in even procession as riders brushed past them on the far side, out of sight.

"I'm finished," Millicent called.

He dropped to the ground and led the Ovaro back to the stream. She'd dried herself. The towel was still in her hand, but she'd hurried and her skin was damp. The yellow blouse clung, emphasizing the curves of her breasts, which were full at the bottom and curved up to tiny, almost nonexistent little points. She followed his gaze, spun away, and climbed onto the gray gelding. "Let's go," she said as she moved into the drying warmth of the sun.

"Not that way," he said. "There are Kiowas up there heading downward." He saw her eyes widen with fright, and she swung in behind him as he moved the Ovaro downward to circle away frm the Indians. He led the way through a stand of thick woodland brush, short, bushy hawthorns and tall hackberries. Then he reined in abruptly. Four Kiowa were coming toward him through the timber, not more than fifty yards away. He saw that the Ovaro and the gelding were hidden by the tops of the hawthorns.

"Down," he hissed to Millicent as he slid from the saddle to flatten himself on the ground. Millicent followed, apprehension deepening the lovely lines of her face. He pulled her down beside him. "Get under me," he said.

"What?" She frowned, immediate protest in her eyes.

"Under me, dammit. Get that yellow blouse out of sight,"

Fargo said as he lifted himself and pulled her onto her back beneath him. He lay down over her, covering the blouse with his chest and arms as the Kiowa drew closer. He watched the four horsemen move still closer, execute a slow turn single file as they followed a narrow path that led past but a scant dozen yards away. Fargo lay hardly breathing. He felt the warm softness of Millicent's breasts press into him, firm yet yielding, and he drank in the sweet woman smell of her. He watched as the Kiowa moved on slowly, disappearing into the trees. He looked down at Millicent. Her blue eyes were round with fright.

"Shhh-h," he whispered, moving slightly but enough to rub his shirt across her breasts. He saw the flush come into her face as he lay over her, exchanging warmth. The flush in her cheeks deepened.

"Have they gone yet?" she whispered.

"No," he answered, barely breathing the word. He moved downward a fraction, rubbing across her breasts. The tiny points seemed to have disappeared altogether, he noticed as he stayed pressed into her. She waited another long minute and he saw her twist her neck around to peer up over her shoulder for the Kiowa. She pulled her head back to him, her frown instant.

"There's nothing there," she said.

"Quiet, they just left," he said. Her eyes were filled with uncertainty, disbelief, and gathering anger as she pushed herself out from under him. He leaned back and rose to his feet as she glared. "You've got to believe in people more, Millie," he remarked.

"Some people make that very difficult," she returned cily as he retrieved the horses.

"We walk for a little while," he said as he continued downhill and in a wide circle. Finally they mounted again and Millicent came alongside him.

"Who are you going to see?" she asked as they rode up the other side of the hill.

"Old friend. Joseph Threehats," he said.

"Joseph Threehats? How did he ever get that name?" Millicent asked.

"His mother was Ojibwa, his father a white trapper," Fargo explained. "When he was born, the chief of his mother's tribe said this child will wear three hats, the Indian's bonnet, the white man's hat, and his own, and so he will be called Joseph Threehats."

"Why do I get the feeling you're going to him for help with the Kiowa, not for Mai-lin?" she asked.

"Because you've a suspicious nature, Millie," he answered.

"Millicent," she snapped. "Where does this Joseph Threehats live?" she asked.

"In a wickiup, alone, with an ocassional woman. He roams around, watches, listens, absorbs. Damn little goes on that he doesn't get wind of somewhere, someplace. He can talk white man and he can talk Indian, but more important, he can think white man and think Indian."

"How does he make money to live?"

"He doesn't need much money. When he does, he'll scout for the army and they'll be grateful. He's the best there is," Fargo said.

"How much farther?" she asked.

"Other side of the next hill," he told her, and spurred the Ovaro into a canter. She caught up to him as he crested the hill and paused to sweep the terrain with a long glance. Satisfied, he headed downward as Millicent rode beside him. The sun made her almost blond hair a soft gold, he noted, and as she leaned back in the saddle while the gray went downhill, her breasts pushed up deliciously into the yellow blouse. She saw his glance, tried to sit up straighter

d slid forward in the saddle. He laughed as she had to
an back again. She tossed a glare at him.

The wickiup came into sight at the top of the next slope. It
as built of earth and twigs and a few stones. Joseph had
dded a small, three-sided thatched-roof stable to the back
f it, Fargo noted.

He rode down the slope and swung from the saddle
efore the Ovaro had come to a full halt in front of the wick-
p. Joseph stepped from the open, low-roofed doorway, his
und face breaking into a wide grin. "Fargo, fellah," he
lled out. "Damn time you come 'round."

Fargo returned the warm handshake and tossed a glance
Millicent as she pulled up to a halt. He smiled inwardly at
e disappointment and dismay that touched her face as she
ok in Joseph Threehat's slight paunch under the dun-
lored shirt that he wore outside his trousers. She didn't
em to like much better the black, battered stetson atop
s head nor the bland face that resembled a crinkled moon
ith small, black eyes.

"Joseph, this is Millicent," Fargo said. He watched
seph Threehats' small, black eyes take in her straight,
mrod figure and caught the amusement that flickered in
eir ebony depths.

"Fargo's woman always welcome here," Joseph said.
Good."

"I am not his woman," Millicent protested instantly.

"Not good," Joseph said, and motioned to the wickiup as
illicent dismounted. "Go in. Sit down. Made some good
ang today. I'll get it."

Millicent allowed a polite smile as she stepped inside the
ttle hut. Joseph took Fargo aside to speak in a low mur-
ur. Fargo answered, laughed, and hurried into the wick-
p after Millicent, who turned her eyes on him at once.
here were folded blankets on the floor for seats and a thick
ndle for light. A low table fashioned from the base of a

55

tree trunk took up the center of the single room and
hearth made of stones took up one corner surrounded
iron kettles and skillets.

"He's certainly not what I expected," Millicent said. "H
has less than an impressive appearance."

"True enough. He likes it that way," Fargo answered.

Millicent frowned. "What did he say to you outside?" sl
queried.

"He asked me why you were lying on your back in th
woods." Fargo laughed as Millicent's mouth fell open.

"How did he know that?" she gasped.

"Little pieces of wheatgrass stuck in the back of you
skirt, wrinkles in the back of your blouse with moss stains
Fargo said.

"All right, he's observant. But he's quick to make wroi
assumptions," she sniffed.

"About you being my woman?" Fargo laughed. "He kne
better, but he found out all kinds of things about you just l
the way you answered."

Millicent's eyes narrowed as she stared back and Farg
sat down on one of the folded blankets. Joseph entered tl
wickiup carrying three small clay cups without handle
each filled almost to overflowing. He handed one
Millicent, one to Fargo, and he raised the third one into tl
air.

"To old times and new times," Joseph said.

Fargo raised his cup to his lips and drew in a long sip. H
watched as Millicent took a deep swig. Her cheeks gre
red, the deep flush moving down her throat. A sharp gasp
breath burst from her.

"My God," Millicent whispered. "My God."

"Good bang, eh?" Joseph grinned.

"What . . . what's he talking about?" Millicent rasped
she fought for breath.

"Bang, that's the name of that drink," Fargo said. "Joseph makes his own verison, but it's a good one."

"Bourbon and warm ale, some sugar, nutmeg, ginger, and a jigger of gin," Joseph said. "Damn fine drink." He took another long pull and inhaled with satisfaction as Millicent watched in awe, her face slowly returning to its normal color.

"Damn fine drink, Joseph," Fargo echoed, and took another sip. "Need some help, Joseph. Good pay, army money." Joseph grunted. "Two things, one for the army, one for Millicent, here," Fargo went on, and Joseph sat back on a blanket as his little black eyes questioned. "Ladies, first," Fargo said to Millicent, and he let her tell Joseph about Mai-lin. When she finished, he saw Joseph's eyes go to him. "Ever hear about a slave girl ring here?" Fargo asked.

"Once or twice. Drunk talk in bars," Joseph said.

"No one-shack homesteader. Somebody with money, space, help. Who fits, Joseph?" Fargo asked.

Joseph Threehats half-closed his eyes as he finished the last of his drink. He stayed silent, in a kind of meditation, until he slowly opened his eyes. He spoke softly, thoughtfully. "Thorenson," he said. "Lives a half-dozen miles east of Spineyleaf, at the foothills of the Wasatch. Big house, maybe six, eight hands. Calls himself Trader Thorenson. Whatever you want, he can get for you."

"Including slave girls, perhaps," Millicent said.

"Never heard that, but could be," Joseph said. "He's got plenty mud on his boots."

"Such as?" Fargo questioned.

"Used to trade beef to the army till they found out he was selling them stolen cattle," Joseph said. "He ran beaver trade with the trappers and cheated them blind. He has old silver mine back of his place. Never any good, but he sold

57

stock in it. Lot of people lose their shirts. Been closed down for years, now."

"Trader Thorenson," Fargo echoed, turning the name on his tongue. "Could be our man."

"What's the other?" Joseph asked.

"The Kiowa. Something damn funny going on," Fargo said.

Joseph Threehats listened, his little black eyes sharp, as Fargo spoke in terse, short sentences. There was no need for embroidery, not with Joseph Threehats. When he finished, Joseph's lips pursed in thought. "You right, Fargo. Damn funny," he muttered.

"That chief's name mean anything to you?" Fargo questioned.

"Tarawa, Thunder Chief? Yes, bad medicine. He come up from the Chaco Canyon Kiowa, take charge here," Joseph said.

"Think you can get a handle on what he's up to?" Fargo asked.

"Maybe. Have to ride out, make talk, listen hard," Joseph said.

Fargo pulled the roll of bills the captain had given him from his pocket and handed it to Joseph. "Army pay up front. Get started, Joseph," he said. "We'll be heading back to Spineyleaf."

"I ride a ways with you," Joseph said, rising to his feet and pocketing the roll of bills. "I get my horse." He left the wickiup and Fargo followed him outside with Millicent.

"You didn't tell me the army had paid you," she said.

"Didn't say they hadn't," he answered.

"I'm paying you to find Mai-lin, just remember that," she snapped.

"I don't figure you're going to let me forget it," he said.

Joseph reappeared riding a brown gelding with a white blaze, not a big horse but short-coupled and tightly mus cled, a horse made for any kind of terrain. He carried a small leather-covered jug around the saddle horn and he patted it affectionately.

"Rest of the bang," he said. " 'Case I get thirsty."

"I'm sure you will," Millicent said with disapproval in her voice. She swung onto the dark-gray gelding and Fargo mounted his horse. He watched Joseph's eyes stay on her as she swung alongside the Ovaro.

"You learn riding at girl's school back East," he said.

"Why yes, in fact," Millicent said, surprised again. "How did you know?"

"By how you hold hands and elbows, way you sit on horse," Joseph answered as Fargo led the way up the slope.

"Something wrong with that?" Millicent returned.

"Good rider rides with his horse, not on it," Joseph answered as he broke into a canter. Millicent glared at Fargo as he laughed. Joseph had halted at the crest of the slope when they caught up to him. He pointed west to where the Wasatch Range rose. A mountain pass threaded its way down the nearest part of the range. "China girl come down through that way," Joseph grunted. "Hard way, but safest for them."

"Why?"

"No place for wagons or settlers. Indians not bother watch it," he said.

"Then why don't we just watch that pass?" Millicent asked.

"Six, maybe eight more passes," Joseph grunted, and moved his horse down the other side of the slope.

Fargo drew past him and Millicent fell in close behind as they headed down. Heavy timber covered the slope, but he knew that flat land lay just at the bottom and he led the way through a thick stand of red oak and paper birch. He reined up sharply as he came into the clear. Joseph rode up to follow his eyes as he frowned at the wide wings that wheeled

59

in slow circles through the sky just beyond the next stand of timber.

"Goddamn," Fargo bit out as he sent the Ovaro into a full gallop. He heard Joseph and Millicent following as he raced into the trees, skirted around a line of bur oaks, and ducked his head to pass beneath the low, spreading branches of a box elder. He glimpsed the soaring wings through a break in the trees and cursed again. Their grisly message was always the same.

He sent the Ovaro racing through an opening in the timber and down onto the flat land. The soaring, circling wings became vultures, their featherless, curved-beak heads and huge wingspreads symbols of ugliness. More wings fluttered and rose into the sky as if in protest at his interruption. He reined to a halt and took in the scene in one grim glance. He counted twelve bodies, naked, two of the women scalped, the stench of death and blood under the sun filling the air. Most of the bodies had been partially eaten by the vultures. He heard Millicent's gasp of horror as she came to a halt.

"Oh, my God. I'm going to be sick," she murmured.

"Breathe through your mouth," he said as Joseph came alongside. His bland face had become a round stone, Fargo saw, and his little black eyes moved slowly over the scene.

"You right, Fargo. Something damn funny going on," Joseph hissed. "They take wagons, too."

"Just like the others," Fargo said. He pointed to the other side of the scene where the wagon tracks moved into a bank of trees. Joseph started to go after the tracks and Fargo shot a glance at Millicent. She sat almost doubled over in the saddle, her eyes pressed tightly shut. "That won't make it go away," he said almost harshly. "Once you've seen it it's inside you forever. Ride." He spurred his horse forward to follow Joseph and the wagon tracks. He glanced back at Millicent. She was coming along, riding with her head

verted and her eyes turned away. Fargo rode ahead and
aught up to where Joseph slowly followed the tracks.
They covered the others," Fargo commented. "Not this
me, though."

"Maybe in too big hurry," Joseph offered.

"Maybe something else," Fargo said as he saw the blue
bbon of water through the trees. The wagon tracks rolled
irectly to the bank of a fair-sized river and Joseph halted
eside him.

"River run down from Bear Lake up north," he said.
Deep enough to float wagons."

"And leave no more tracks. They could've gone upriver
r down," Fargo muttered. He was developing a bitter
espect for this Kiowa called Tarawa, Thunder Chief.
Iillicent pulled to a halt. She'd gathered herself into ram-
od stiffness, but her delicately lined face still remained
halk-white.

"I go north here, Fargo," Joseph Threehats said. "Be
ack in few days. I find you in Spineyleaf?"

"Check at the Dobson house. Millie will know where I
n," Fargo said.

Joseph nodded and Fargo met the sober glance Joseph
ssed at him as he rode north along the bank of the river.

4

The gray purple of dusk was sliding fast down the high lan[d]. Fargo turned to Millicent. "Let's go find a spot to mak[e] camp," he said, wheeling the Ovaro.

"Not near here," Millicent said hastily, her voice tigh[t] and he understood. Making a wide circle, they kept ridi[n] as dusk became dark. They finally found a glen beside [a] stream. Millicent dismounted and unsaddled the gray as h[e] made a small fire to warm the beef jerky he took from h[is] saddlebag. She sat across the tiny fire from him, her le[gs] drawn up, arms clasping her knees. He saw her meet h[is] eyes and her lips grow firm.

"It didn't change my mind, horrible as it was, if tha[t's] what you're thinking," she muttered. "Mai-lin comes fir[st] more than ever now. How can anyone live in this land? It'[s a] savage, cruel place."

"It's that, but it's a place of hope, too, and beauty," Farg[o] answered. He offered some of the warmed jerky to her a[nd] she forced herself to eat a little. When he finished, he p[ut] out the fire and rose to his feet. "Get some sleep," he sai[d].

Millicent stood up and went behind her horse to chang[e]. Fargo watched a low moon paint silver tips on the trees

e undressed to his shorts and stretched his magnificently
uscled body. The night had stayed hot, with almost a
oying thickness to the air. Millicent stepped from behind
e gelding in a long dark-green nightdress. She stared at
im.

"Are you going to sleep like that?" she asked, instant dis-
proval in her voice.

"Why not? Feels real nice and cool on a hot night like
is," he said, stretching his arms behind his head.

"Haven't you even pajama trousers?" She frowned.

"Never needed them," he said cheerfully. "Listen, you
n't have to wear that long thing if you don't want to.
ooks real hot," he said sympathetically.

"It's just fine, thank you," Millicent sniffed as she settled
rself on the grass with a blanket for a pillow. She lay with
r back to him and he stayed stretched out. He closed his
es, apparently asleep but actually listening, his wild-
eature hearing picking up every night sound. Deer passed
arby with careful steps. A pair of raccoons chattered in
e distance. But the sound he had listened for finally came
Millicent turned, the faint rustle of the nightdress
ifting through the dark. He picked up the sound of a small
ne rolling away as she raised herself on one elbow. He
d not move. He could feel her eyes moving up and down
s body. Her breath grew shallower. He smiled inwardly
d wagered it was the first time she'd had the chance to
ok at a man's near-naked body. He moved one leg slowly,
if in sleep, and knew the bulge at the crotch of his shorts
s now more prominent. He heard her breathing halt for a
oment, and then resume with a slow, shallow gasp. He lay
ll and finally heard her sink down on the grass and turn,
d when he opened his eyes a fraction, she lay with her
ck to him. He smiled again, but not inwardly this time.
ery filly took different handling. Some just took more
an others to bring around.

He closed his eyes and slept, the night undisturbed, an woke with the new warmth of the sun. He rose, washed i the little stream, and pulled on clothes as he looked acros at Millicent. The nightdress had ridden up as she slept t reveal a long, nicely turned calf, the back of one knee, and flash of thigh. She heard him at the stream, turned awake and quickly pulled the nightdress down. He turned, sac dled the Ovaro as she washed and again used the gray t change. He watched her as she emerged, brushing he almost blond hair. He waited till she washed at the strear and finished saddling her horse.

"You took longer than I thought you would last night," h remarked casually.

"Longer at what?" She frowned.

"Looking," he said, and watched her face grow brigh red, the color creeping down her neckline.

"I didn't look at anything. You were asleep," she saie "You must have been dreaming."

"I wasn't the one dreaming, honey." He laughed as h swung onto the Ovaro. "Let's ride, Millie." He sent th horse off in a fast trot, then slowed and let her catch up him. She rode in simmering silence as he led the wa toward Spineyleaf. They had come down to fairly flat lar when the line of six uniformed troopers crossed their path Captain Rogers riding lead. His grim face and the dir stained boots of his men spoke clearly enough.

"Saw them just before sundown," Fargo said as the ca tain halted.

"They were on their way to Fort Calder," the capta said. "I spoke to them a few days back." His lips pulled ba and he pounded his fist against the saddle. "Goddamn, I' always too late," he cried out with despair and anger.

"Can't blame yourself for that," Fargo said. "Won't he any. I might have some answers soon."

Captain Rogers nodded and his glance at Millie held in

on. "This isn't my idea of scouting the Kiowa, Fargo," he
l.

"Man needs some relaxation," Fargo said, and saw
llicent's lips come open in protest. But the captain
tioned his troopers on and cantered away.

"How dare you?" Millicent flung at Fargo as the line of
opers receded. "You let him think—"

"I know what I let him think," Fargo interrupted harshly.

"Why didn't you tell him what I'm doing here?" she
nanded.

"And let his squad hear?" Fargo snapped. "It'd be saloon
k by tonight, and talk travels fast. You want to catch a fox,
1 don't tell him you're coming."

Her glare faded into a half-pout. "You could've thought of
nething else to tell him," she said. "I object to being
en for one of your bedmates."

"Just think how much more fun you'd be having if you
re." He grinned.

She turned away with her chin high and he moved the
aro forward. She rode in silence until they reached
ineyleaf. "What now?" she asked.

"You go to the house and stay there. I'll check around
ne about Willie Rank," he said.

"Let me know what you find out," she ordered.

He ignored the demand in her tone as he moved on. He
ided to start at the most likely place, the blacksmith
p. He found a burly man in a leather apron pounding his
il. The smithy looked up as the magnificent Ovaro came
a halt outside his shop, his eyes taking in the horse with
e knowing glance.

"Mighty fine animal, mister," the smithy said.

"Thank you." Fargo nodded. "I'm looking for Willie
nk. You know him?"

"I might," the man said. "What do you want with
llie?"

"I was told he does odd jobs," Fargo said smoothly.

The blacksmith threw his head back as he let out a boo‐
ing laugh. "Willie Rank work?" he said. "Never heard of
mister."

"I'll give it a try," Fargo said.

"Got to find him sober, first," the smithy said.

"Willie Rank doesn't work but he has plenty of money
booze?" Fargo queried.

"Always has had," the smithy said. "Somebody keeps h
supplied."

"Got any idea who?"

"None." The blacksmith shrugged.

"Where can I find Willie?" Fargo asked, still keeping
tone casual.

"He lives just north of town, an old, deserted grain wa
house," the blacksmith said. "Good luck, but don't exp
too much."

"I won't," Fargo said. "Thanks." He moved the ho
slowly up the street, headed north through town, and wh
he reached the outskirts of Main Street, he spotted a lo
wooden structure with one end almost collapsed onto its
He dismounted and stepped to a door more off its hin
than on.

"Willie?" Fargo called as he pushed the door open, taki
care not to knock it from its precarious position. He stepp
into the old granary and the stale smell of dank air, tobac
and whiskey filled his nostrils. "Willie?" he called again
he started along the length of the abandoned structure. O
wall was lined high with broken boxes, crates, and old b
rels, the other with what once had been grain bins but we
now empty, broken stalls. Four windows, boarded up a
near the roofline, filled the opposite wall. He glimps
another door on the far side of the structure. "Willie Ran
he called again. Only the scurrying sound of a wood
answered.

66

He walked past an out-of-order millstone to the other end
the structure. There were a cot and blankets, an
lighted candle, a bundle of old clothes, a half-dozen tins
tobacco, and dozens of empty whiskey bottles piled high
one corner. Willie lived in something less than high
le, he grunted wryly. Fargo moved carefully, taking care
t to disturb anything. He'd seen derelicts before that
ew exactly the order of their disorder.

But he read the clutter much as he read a mountain trail,
th the probing eye of the trailsman where everything said
mething. Willie Rank lived alone, did no cooking and pre-
us little washing. There wasn't a clean shirt or clothesline
the place. More important, he was a solitary drinker. The
llection of empty whiskey bottles gave evidence of that.
ost drunks were barflies, scrounging and consuming their
uor at the local saloon. Willie Rank was a kept man,
rgo mused, kept in booze so he'd be on hand when
eded. A private courier kept in place.

Fargo turned and made his way back through the aban-
ned old granary. He pulled the door carefully closed after
m and swung onto the Ovaro. He rode some twenty yards
a low-branched, wide box elder and positioned himself
hind the tree trunk. Dismounting, he sat down to take up
tch. He stayed beneath the big tree through the after-
on. Willie Rank failed to appear. Had he gone to get his
pply of booze money, Fargo pondered, or was he earning
s keep delivering messages? Dusk became dark and Fargo
se, pulled himself into the saddle, and headed the horse
ward town. Millicent was the kind who'd lose patience
ickly. She'd come looking for him in the dark and he
dn't want that. He didn't aim to humor her by reporting
, but he wanted to keep her out of his hair. Willie Rank
uld return, he was certain, and he wanted a free hand
th the man without having to be concerned about
illicent. So he rode directly to the small white house.

Millicent opened the door as he dismounted, her brillia‐
blue eyes crackling with questions. As he stepped into t‐
house, he told her what he'd learned about Willie Ran‐
Her eyes were triumphant as he finished. "It all fits. He h‐
to be the courier. He's being kept on call. Trader Thore‐
son?" she offered.

"Could be." Fargo shrugged. "Could be somebody els‐
too."

"We'll keep watching Willie Rank's place tonight‐
Millicent said.

"We won't do anything tonight. You stay put here," Far‐
said.

"I'll do no such thing," she snapped.

Fargo started to answer but held back. He'd be damm‐
if he'd bring her along, he muttered inwardly, but he did‐
want to clash with her headstrong stubborn ideas.

"I'm not watching Willie tonight. He'll keep, now tha‐
know where to find him," Fargo said.

"I think we ought to keep watching his place tonigh‐
she insisted.

"In time. I want to check out some other things tonigh‐
Fargo said evenly.

"What things?" she asked suspiciously.

"Tell you when I've something to say," Fargo sai‐
"Tomorrow."

Her eyes peered at him, uncertainty and suspicion‐
their blue depths. "I told you, Fargo, I don't intend to ‐
kept on the sidelines." She frowned.

"Wouldn't think of it." He smiled agreeably. It did‐
erase the suspicion in her eyes as he opened the door a‐
stepped outside. "Just want to follow up on a few things. ‐
report to you, come morning. Promise," he said. ‐
mounted the Ovaro and waved to her as she stood in t‐
doorway, pensive. He turned the horse south, aware t‐

er eyes followed him until he disappeared into the darkness.

Once beyond town, he made a wide circle into the low hills and looped back north until he halted beneath the low-branched box elder once again. He dismounted, peered through the night at the old granary; it was but a long, dark shape in the dark. He settled down against the tree trunk in that state of relaxed alertness he had long ago mastered, a kind of quiet suspension of the body that freed the senses. He guessed that perhaps two hours had passed when he saw the soft glow of yellow light in one corner of the old warehouse.

He rose, peered into the dark. His eyes hadn't played tricks, the glow remained, flickering through the cracked wooden planks of the abandoned structure. A candle burned inside. Willie Rank had returned and slipped inside in the darkness.

Fargo moved from beneath the box elder with long-legged strides, leading the Ovaro behind him. He left the horse alongside a tall bush near the old granary and reached the door in another half-dozen long strides. Pressing both hands against the door, he inched it open silently until he could slip inside. The candlelight flickered dimly at the far end of the long corridor, which ran down the center of the old warehouse. He moved in a crouch between the rows of stacked crates and empty grain bins. The candlelight grew brighter and he found a place where he could slide behind one of the grain bins. He moved along the wall and brushed aside a spider web that clung to his face as he moved through the narrow space behind the bin. The corner of the granary came into view, the candle burning brightly. Willie Rank stepped into his line of vision. Fargo saw a tall, thin frame with high shoulders, wearing Levi's and a dirty gray shirt. Unkempt black hair hung down around a sunken-cheeked face with hollow eye sockets. It was a face that

could have been embalmed, because of the network o
liquor-reddened tiny veins that ran through it. Black eye
and a turned-down, mean mouth completed Willie Rank
gaunt appearance. Fargo heard the man curse as h
attacked the huge pile of empty whiskey bottles. He picke
up bottle after bottle, tilting each to see if a drop were lef
He then threw each aside in angry disgust. He attacked th
pile of bottles with the frenzy of an alcoholic denied an
desperate.

Fargo's eyes narrowed in thought as he watched. Th
implications were plain enough. Willie Rank had gone off t
get his liquor money and had come back without it. Who
ever kept him wanted him sober for a few days. Sober so h
could receive and deliver a message? Fargo let the though
hang for a moment. It meant that some kind of word wa
expected soon. He continued to watch Willie attack th
stack of empty whiskey bottles. He had just decided it wa
time to get some proper answers out of Willie Rank whe
the old granary erupted with the sound of toppling crate
and barrels.

He dropped to one knee, an instant reaction, the Colt i
his hand at once, his eyes on the barrels and crates tha
spilled across the floor. He saw Willie spin to see it also
Fargo grimaced and repressed the curse welling up insid
him as, along with the crates and barrels, a figure fell int
the open. The candlelight highlighted the almost blond ha
first, and then the fine-lined face, filled with alarm and cha
grin. He saw Willie move with surprising speed, leap fo
ward to clamp one hand around Millicent's wrist as she la
sprawled on the floor.

"What are you doin' in here?" the man snarled as h
yanked her to her feet. "Come in spyin' on me, did you?" h
said, twisting her wrist.

Millicent cried out in pain as he spun her around.

Fargo cursed silently. She had sneaked into the granar

om the other side, probably hours back, he reckoned. Willie's snarl broke into his thoughts again. "I said what're ou doin' in here?" the man demanded, and twisted her rist again.

Millicent found words between her cries of pain. "I came here because I'd no place else to stay," she said.

Willie Rank rejected the answer instantly. "Liar. You ome here spyin' on me," he hissed. "Why? Who the hell re you?" He twisted hard on her wrist again and Millicent asped. "Who are you, bitch?" Willie snarled.

Fargo moved forward, the big Colt in his hand. "A damn ol, pain-in-the ass girl," he said. "And you let go of her, Villie."

Willie spun to face him but kept his grip on Millicent's eck as he stared with anger and surprise at the new truder. "Goddamn," Willie Rank hissed. "Another one."

Fargo saw his hand go to his trouser pocket and the knife ppeared at once, the point of the blade pressed against Millicent's neck.

"One wrong move and I'll stick it right through her," Villie Rank growled. Fargo saw his eyes go to the big Colt nd Willie shifted the knife so the edge of the blade pressed cross Millicent's throat. "The gun . . . throw it over here. ow, or you can have her head," he snarled.

Fargo measured the distance and his lips drew back in ustration. Willie Rank was almost completely hidden ehind Millicent, a shot too great to risk. "The gun, oddammit," Willie shouted. Fargo delayed a moment ore, his gaze on the knife held across Millicent's throat. The ightest pressure and the blade would slice through her gular. Willie Rank's hand trembled. He could do it by ccident.

Fargo cursed silently as he lowered his gun and sent it kidding across the floor toward Willie Rank. He watched as

71

the Colt struck one of the warped old floorboards, leap
sideways, spun, and skittered against the wall.

Willie Rank cursed, sent Millicent sprawling with a
shove, and dived for the gun. He realized his mistake in
judgment as the big black-haired man moved with the
speed of a puma striking. Fargo bowled into him broadside
and Willie Rank flew sideways to crash into the wall. Fargo
reached for the tall, thin figure and pulled back as Willie
Rank lashed out, the knife slicing through the air.

Willie rolled, came up on his feet, and jabbed with the
knife. Fargo backed up, glimpsed Millicent to one side, her
eyes wide as she watched the battle. Willie, his lips drawn
tight, lunged again with the knife, his movements surpris-
ingly quick. Fargo pulled away from one lunge, ducked
another, and watched as Willie slashed with the blade
again. Willie had a pattern to his moves, Fargo saw with
narrowed eyes. He slashed upward first, followed with a
straight lunge, and then a downward slash. Fargo half
circled and Willie followed. "I'll kill you, mister," the man
snarled and Fargo gave ground, letting Willie come at him
again. Willie slashed upward, then straight, then downward. Fargo avoided the third slash and moved forward to
bring his fist down, using all the strength in his shoulder
muscles. The blow smashed against the top of Willie Rank's
hand with the force of a sledgehammer. Willie cursed in
pain as the knife fell from his fingers. Fargo's left caught
Willie in the ribs. He grunted and doubled over, and
Fargo's short, looping right smashed into his jaw.

Willie flew up and backward, smashing into the thick candle. Fargo saw the burning wick catapult into the air and
land on a pile of dirty, alcohol-stained clothes. The sheet of
fire seemed to explode into the air as Willie Rank regained
his feet. Fargo saw tongues of flame leap onto the tinder-
dry, old wood of the granary; in seconds, one wall became a
tower of flame. Years of dry dust exploded all over into littl

lls of fire that swept upward along the wooden beams.
rgo glanced to one side and saw Millicent backed against
e of the grain bins before the smash of glass brought his
es back to Willie. The man came at him with a jagged
ece of broken bottle in one hand, and once more Fargo
cled and backed up. Now he felt the heat of the flames.
e ducked as Willie lunged with the jagged bottle, upward
d forward. Despite the new weapon, his attack pattern
mained the same, and Fargo set himself for the third
rust. It came at once, a downward arc, and Fargo held his
ound as long as he dared, then twisted sideways. He felt
e jagged piece of glass graze his arm. He swung with all
s strength, using both fists as one, and smashed a tremen-
us blow to Willie's kidney. Willie Rank half-screamed,
lf-gasped as he fell sprawling facedown, the broken piece
bottle rolling to the side.

Fargo started after him, ducked as a wild tongue of flame
pt out from the nearest wall. The flame shot upward and
rgo moved in a crouch. He grasped Willie's feet and
agged him to the center of the floor. Willie lay with his
s drawn up in pain, gasping to regain his breath. Fargo
ked across the room to see Millicent half-falling forward
the grain bin behind her went up in flames. "Over here,"
shouted above the noise of the fire, now a crackling, roar-
inferno as the entire old building began to go up, the dry
od burning as though it were paper. A spiral of flame on
e wall broke in two and parted, and Fargo spied his Colt
inst the wall. He dropped to his stomach and used his
ows to propel himself across the floor in a fast crawl. He
t the searing blast of heat as he neared the flaming wall,
t one long arm out, and got his hand around the butt of
gun. He yanked it toward him as he scooted backward
b-fashion, ducking his head away from a blast of fire that
ped toward him

He reached the center of the floor where Willie had

regained enough breath to rise to his hands and knees, h
sunken face still distorted with pain. Millicent crouche
beside him, her frightened gaze scanning the flaming wal
"The side door, where you sneaked in," Fargo said to he

"That way," she said, pointing to a narrow place behi
where the barrels had tumbled. The wood was smoking b
hadn't blazed into flame yet. She started for the spot a
Fargo closed one hand around Willie Rank's neck a
pushed him forward. He'd reached the narrow passagew
behind the clutter of crates when the opposite wall ca
down, taking a part of the roof with it.

"Down," he yelled at Millicent as he threw himself f
ward onto the floor half over Willie. The ball of sparks a
burning bits of wood blew over them, the searing heat o
singing his forehead. The inside of the old granary seem
made of hanging bits of flame that circled into the updraft
air. "Keep going," he yelled, and Millicent rose, stumbli
forward. The smoke began to grow thick, and Millicent va
ished for a moment, reappearing as she reached the si
door. Fargo saw her push it outward and half-fall into t
night. He propelled Willie ahead of him and ducked a pie
of beam that toppled in flames an inch from his should
He reached the door and pushed Willie out into the nig
flung him to the ground as he fell onto one knee and hea
the harsh sound of his own breath.

Millicent sat on the ground, gasping. Fargo turned to s
the entire back half of the old granary enveloped in flam
shooting skyward, tainting the blackness with an oran
glow. They'd see it in Spineyleaf now and half the to
would be on its way in minutes. He pulled himself to
feet, the Colt leveled at Willie. "Get up," he ordered.

Willie Rank turned, rose, and leapt at him, a snarl dra
ing his lips back to make his sunken face into somethi
resembling a gargoyle.

"Goddamn," Fargo swore as he held his finger back

74

e trigger. He wanted Willie alive, able to answer ques-
ns. He drew his arm back as Willie slammed into him,
ove a short blow into the thin frame just over the
dsection. He heard the man grunt in pain as he fell to one
ee. Fargo started to bring the Colt down onto his temple,
t Willie Rank, fighting out of some wild sense of despera-
n, got his arm up and deflected the blow. He closed one
nd around the Colt and Fargo saw him raise his head,
en his mouth and start to sink his teeth into the hand
lding the gun.

"Son of a bitch," Fargo swore as he could only pull his
nd away to avoid the bite. The Colt fell to the ground and
illie dived for it, falling atop it. As Willie grasped the gun,
rgo kicked at his elbow. But the kick landed on his fore-
n, sending his arm snapping upward as he pulled the trig-
r. The Colt roared and Fargo saw the heavy bullet tear up
ough Willie Rank's chin. His face split apart in two red-
shing halves.

"My God," Fargo heard Millicent cry out as Willie Rank
emed to stare out of disconnected eyes for a final moment
d then his long frame crumpled to the ground. "Oh, my
d," Millicent echoed in a choked gasp.

"Shit," Fargo swore as he pulled his Colt away from the
eless fingers. He turned as his ears picked up the distant
nd of shouts. The town was on its way, dammit, he
anted silently. He shot an angry glance at Millicent as he
ked up Willie Rank's lifeless form by one arm and a leg.

"What are you doing?" Millicent asked as he strode to the
ge of the flaming granary, the entire building now envel-
ed in leaping tongues of fire. He swung Willie's long
dy in a half-arc and threw it into the burning warehouse.
rror poured into Millicent's eyes. He yanked her by the
nd as he ran to where he'd left the Ovaro.

"We get away from here first and talk later," he said. He

reached the Ovaro in half-a-dozen strides. "You come ⟨
horse?" He glared at Millie.

She nodded. "He's tied around the other side."

"Get him, dammit. *Fast*," Fargo bit out, and Mill⟩
started to race around to the far side of the flaming stru⟨
ture. The shouts and voices were clear now. The crowd v⟨
coming fast. He waited till Millicent appeared on the gr⟨
before he swung into the saddle. She came up close behi⟨
him as he galloped up the slope to halt under the big b⟨
elder. Millicent reined up still staring with horror at hi⟨
He answered the unstated questions through tight lips th⟨
barely moved. "If he was found outside and shot, there'd ⟨
questions. The wrong people might start wondering abo⟨
it," Fargo said. "This way they'll find damn little left of h⟨
when the fire dies down. They'll just figure he was booz⟨
up as usual and set the place and himself on fire."

Millicent blinked, nodded, and let her shoulders relax ⟨
she drew in a deep sigh. "You do think ahead, I must say⟨
she commented.

"Right now I'm thinking ahead to fanning your little as⟨
Fargo bit out. "You had one lead and you blew it."

"It was an accident. One of those old boards gave way a⟨
I fell," Millicent said.

"It wouldn't have given way if you hadn't been the⟨
standing on it. I told you to stay in the goddamn house⟨
Fargo roared back.

Millicent drew her lips in tight. "It was your own faul⟨
she said loftily

"My fault? Jesus, now I've heard everything," Far⟨
threw back.

"You shouldn't have lied to me. You said you were ⟨
going to watch him tonight," she answered

"Just so you wouldn't pull anything stupid, which y⟨
went ahead and did anyway, dammit," Fargo returne⟨

Now we've got nothing. You happy with your bonehead lay?"

"You shouldn't have lied to me," she said truculently.

"I should've tied you up," Fargo said. "Now I've got to gure a reason for paying Trader Thorenson a visit."

"I've been thinking about that," Millicent said. "Suppose were out here from an eastern riding school looking for orses? I could say I heard he dealt in all kinds of things."

Fargo let his lips purse in thought. "Might work. I'll sleep n it. Meet me here in the morning," he said, and fastened er with a hard stare. "You think you can follow orders long ough to do that?" he stabbed.

"Quite." She glared back

"Stay away from the fire. Make a wide circle and go into wn from the other end," he said.

She started to wheel the gray around and paused. "You uld see me back," she said.

"Why? You'll be safe between here and town," he swered.

"It's called being a gentleman," she sniffed.

"I saved your ass. That ought to make me a gentleman. r a damn fool," he growled.

Millicent's full ruby lips pressed against each other as she nt the gray into a gallop. He watched her disappear into e darkness before he let the little laugh escape him.

5

The morning sun bathed the land in gold as Fargo return
to the low-branched box elder. He'd camped the nig
higher up in the hills and had slept well before making I
way down with the new day. A distant plume of thin smo
marked the night. Fargo dismounted, had just sat down
the dew-covered grass when he saw Millicent ride in
sight. She wore a tailored black jacket over a white sh
open at the neck, a red kerchief tied under the collar, and
tailored black riding skirt. Beautifully elegant, she w
every bit the proper eastern young lady. His eyes admitt
her cool loveliness, but his voice growled.

"Pretty damn sure of yourself, aren't you?" he said.
said I'd sleep on that idea."

"I assumed you had, and realized it is as good an approa
as any," she said crisply. "Shall we go?"

He let silence agree and swung onto the Ovaro to lead tl
way down onto flat land. He rode with his eyes scanning tl
nearby hills and the timber stands that covered the fl
land. They'd traveled a half-hour when he saw a handful
Conestogas in the far distance, almost at the horizon lin

oving from east to west. He steered the Ovaro toward the
aravan. "Where are you going?" Millicent asked sharply.

"To talk to that train," he said.

"It's out of our way," she said.

"Thorenson will keep," he said.

"You don't know that. Every minute is important if we're
oing to find out anything. Mai-lin could be here already or
ue any time soon," Millicent said

"You coming?" he muttered as he rode on. She caught up
him in a few moments and he cast a hard glance at her.
ou've got a short memory," he muttered.

"No, I remember that scene all too well. God, I'll never
rget it. But Mai-lin still comes first. She was more than my
upil for three years. She was a friend, almost like a
unger sister. She comes first. You could try to understand
at," Millicent said.

"I'll work on it," Fargo murmured, his handsome,
tense face expressionless. His path brought him across the
agon train's slow progress, and he halted as the lead
agon pulled to a halt. His lake-blue eyes scanned the other
agons as they rolled up. Families all, with plenty of young-
ers, he observed. Farmers, hoes and rakes pressed to the
des of each wagon.

" 'Morning," the man driving lead wagon called out, a
attered straw hat sitting atop a gray-bearded, lined face. A
oman wearing a gray bonnet and gray dress sat alongside
m.

" 'Morning," Fargo said. "The Kiowa have been hitting
agon trains. Thought you ought to know."

"Much obliged," the man said. "We'll have two men ride
otgun with each wagon. We heard the army patrolled this
rritory."

"Yes and no," Fargo said, and the man frowned. "Too
uch territory, too little army," he said.

The man nodded gravely. "Thanks again, mister," h
said.

"Keep alert," Fargo said as he nodded to the woman an
sent the Ovaro on in a trot. Millicent came alongside him
he returned to their first path. He slowed when the ranch
house came into sight. "You got your words straight in you
mind?" Fargo asked her.

"Perfectly," she said, and he grunted. She had a way
answering that could make one feel reprimanded for asking
The ranchhouse was low-roofed and not very large. Farg
saw four corrals flanking the house, all empty save for one
which held a half-dozen mules. A number of small shed
dotted the land around the house, one with its door ope
revealing sacks of potatoes almost spilling from it. Thre
horsemen came from behind a stable and blocked the wa
hard-eyed men with tight-jawed faces

"Hold it right there," one in a brown leather vest sai
gray eyes flickering over the girl and the big black-hair
man.

"I've come to see Trader Thorenson," Millicent said wit
almost regal command in her tone.

"Wait here," the man said, and rode back to th
ranchhouse while the other two stayed, their eyes mostly
Millicent, Fargo noted. He saw other men appear, two
the stable door, two more from behind one of the litt
sheds. They stayed in place, watching. The brown-veste
figure returned and backed his horse to one side. "Go on
he said, and Fargo followed behind Millicent as she rode u
to the ranchhouse and dismounted. He had just slid fro
his horse when a tall man appeared in the doorway of th
house. He had brown hair flecked with gray, and he w
pushing forty, perhaps, though he was well-built, wit
broad shoulders and a thick neck. He had a square, bloc
like face, a prominent nose, short hair, and a mouth th
belonged on a different face, with soft, thick, fleshy lips

"You wanted to see me?" the man asked, his eyes on Millicent's elegant loveliness with obvious appreciation.

"If you're Trader Thorenson." She smiled coolly.

"I am," the man said.

"I'm Millicent Madison," she said, and gestured to the big man beside her. "This is Fargo, my guide."

Trader Thorenson's glance at Fargo was quick but encompassing. "Come inside," he said, and Fargo fell in behind Millicent as she followed the man into a large living room that took up half the low-roofed house. It would have seemed larger were it not for the clutter of furniture, blankets, old vases in one corner, another piled with furs. "What can I do for you?" Thorenson said to Millie as he gestured to a wicker chair that was free of clutter.

Millicent seated herself almost primly. "I was told in town that you might be able to help me. I'm looking to buy a string of cow ponies to take back to Boston. I work for the Boston Ladies Riding School."

Trader Thorenson nodded, but Fargo saw his eyes study Millicent. "Now, why would you be wanting western cow ponies for an eastern riding school?" he asked.

Millicent let him have another sweet smile. "We decided they'd be a smashing success. Everyone has eastern saddle horses, Morgans, hackneys, Arabians, light harness. We just know we'd be swamped with applicants if we offered something different," she said. "Such as real western cow ponies."

She smiled again and Fargo watched Thorenson nod approvingly. Millicent could spin a very smooth set of lies. He'd learned that already, Fargo reminded himself.

"I'll want some twenty horses," Millicent went on. "All properly saddle-trained. No broncs, understood?" The man nodded again. As Millicent started to talk price, Fargo tuned out Millicent's voice and looked beyond the large room to a hallway. He spotted a kitchen at the far end and

81

two smaller rooms branching off on each side. The interior of the house offered little else and he turned his attention back to the conversation as Thorenson answered Millie.

"Take maybe a month," he said. "Got some other business to take care of first. But I can get your horses for you."

Millicent let disappointment cloud her face. "A month? I'd hoped it would be not more than ten days or so," she said.

"Not likely." Thorenson smiled. "But I'll try. Where do I find you, Miss Madison?"

"I've other things to do, so I'll be traveling. I can stop in next week and find out how you're doing. I'm prepared to pay a bonus for time," Millicent said.

"Good. I'll do the best I can," the man said as Millicent rose to her feet.

"Got a question for you," Fargo spoke up, and Thorenson turned his eyes on him. "Know somebody looking to mine silver. I saw a boarded-up mine shaft just north of here in the Wasatch foothills. Know anything about it?"

"It's mine," Trader Thorenson said.

Fargo let his brows lift in surprise. "Yours? Well, now this friend of mine sort of specializes in old mines other folk have given up on," Fargo said. He saw the man rise to the bait the way a Mississippi card shark moves when he spots an easy mark.

"Well, I didn't give up on it. I'm sure there's big load down deep, but I just didn't have the money left to dig that deep," he said. "A man with money for good equipment would find it."

"I'll tell him to come see you," Fargo said. "Maybe you can work out a deal."

"Not for a month," the man put in hastily. "As I told Miss Madison, I've other businsss to take care of first."

"A month. I'll tell him," Fargo said as he followed Millicent from the house, his eyes sweeping the sheds and corrals again, missing nothing. The extra hands had increased by four more men, he noted as he mounted and rode away a few paces behind Millicent. He brought his horse up beside her only when they were out of sight of the ranchhouse.

"I'd say it went perfectly. He believed every word of it," Millicent said with smug satisfaction.

"Probably," Fargo allowed. "You did well."

"Compliments? How refreshing," she said tartly.

"You earn them, you get them," he said.

"You see what you were looking for?" she asked.

"Enough to know he's not running any slave-girl ring here," Fargo said.

"He has all those outbuildings and little sheds," Millicent said.

"All too much in the open. Somebody stumbles onto the place and a girl yells, he's in trouble. There's no cellar to the house either. I checked that. The walls just go down to the floorboards," Fargo said.

"You saying he's not our man?" Millicent asked.

"No, I'd guess he is," Fargo answered. "Most traders don't post guards to stop visitors. Then he put off getting the horses to you for a month. Hell, he should be able to round up twenty cow ponies in a week, even if he has to buy or steal them. One thing more. He took that bait I tossed him about a buyer for that worthless mine. But he backed off on that for a month, too. It's plain he expects something to keep him busy for the next few weeks at least."

"Such as a shipment of slave girls," Millicent said through tightened lips. "But if not at his place, where?"

"I want to take a look at that old mine of his, come night," Fargo said.

"I'll go with you," she said, and he let his stare answer. "Last night was an accident. You never had an accident?" he accused.

"I've had them," he admitted. "But you stay in the house
I expect Joseph will be trying to find me. I want you there i
he does,"

She said nothing more till they came within sight o
Spineyleaf. "All right, this time," she muttered. "But I tol
you, I'm not being kept on the sidelines."

"I heard you the first time," Fargo said. She started t
move on when his voice halted her. "You forgot to than!
me," he said.

"For what?" she frowned.

"Saving your ass last night," he said. "It's called being
lady." He grinned as he saw her lovely face flush, the bril
liant blue eyes darkening.

"*Touché*," she said. "That's French for your point. .
lapse of good manners on my part."

"I'll take care of that for you, Millie," he said. He leane
over, circled her waist with one big hand, and pulled he
half out of the saddle as he pressed his mouth on hers. H
drank in the soft, warm sweetness of her lips, the feel of he
waist under his hand. Taken by surprise, her full lips staye
half-parted as he pressed harder. He felt her start to tighte
her lips, pause, let him press her mouth open a fractio
wider. The tip of his tongue touched her upper lip befor
she gasped and wrenched herself away.

"That was neither called for nor good manners,
Millicent said, glaring.

"Matter of opinion." He laughed as he turned the Ova
away and took off in a trot. He heard her spur her gray o
and he slowed, turned to watch her ride from sight in he
elegant black riding outfit. He rode on into the hills an
halted for a lunch of hardtack and wild plums, but he ke
tasting the sweetness of soft, ruby lips. He had just finishe
eating when he saw the triangular yellow platoon flag an
the thin line of troopers come into sight. He rode out t

meet Captain Rogers and saw the horses lathered and still breathing hard.

"Kiowa, a dozen of them," the captain said, his face strained. "They kept running, wouldn't turn to fight."

"They're under orders to stay clear of you," Fargo commented. "Probably don't want to risk men or time."

"Got anything for me?" the captain asked.

"Maybe tonight," Fargo said.

"Christ, I hope so," the captain said as he wiped his brow with the sleeve of his uniform. "Got word from Bill Schoonmaker. They found a couple dozen bodies, naked, wagons gone, same scene."

"Up by the Wind River Range?" Fargo asked, and the captain nodded. "I'll come see you tomorrow," Fargo said as Captain Rogers waved his nine troopers forward. Fargo waited till they'd gone from sight, then he slowly circled into the hills until he found a spot and halted. He let the dusk slide across the land and watched as the gray-purple turned black and the stars appeared like magic in the velvet sky. A half-moon hung low and Fargo started to head back toward the Wasatch foothills. He stayed in the hills above Trader Thorenson's and saw light flicker from the ranchhouse far below. He reached the Wasatch foothills and rode diagonally across their sloping soil. He had to search the hills for almost an hour before he came upon the old mine, its main shaft entrance boarded up with crisscrossed planks.

He moved the Ovaro around to the rear of a ledge behind the shaft entrance and out of sight. He dismounted and crouched as he surveyed the area. There was no guard and he moved forward in a crouch until he reached the shaft entrance. His gaze fastened on the ground near the entranceway to the main shaft, the half-moon casting just enough light for him to see. Hoofprints and footprints mingled on the ground and he ran his fingers over the marks. He frowned. Too many prints for a deserted mine entrance, too many and too fresh, he muttered silently. He rose and took hold of the boards nailed across the entranceway to the main shaft. They moved as a unit at his touch. He pulled again and they came open with ease. They had been placed over the entranceway, not boarded over it.

He held the boards open wide enough to slip into the entranceway. The dark of the shaft was total, almost physical in its inky blackness. He halted his own breathing to listen but the shaft returned only the deepest silence. He started to turn back to push the boards aside when he heard the sound of hoofbeats. He ducked down behind the crossed boards and pressed himself against the side of the shaft in the inky blackness. He peered out between the boards and saw two riders come into view and slowly ride past the entranceway. The two men glanced almost idly at the boards as they rode on and he listened as they half-circled the far side of the hill, then retunred and cantered away.

Fargo rose and pushed his way from the mine entrance, a frown still creasing his brow. The two men hadn't simply happened by—they were making a routine check. He filed the fact away as he walked to the place where he'd hidden the Ovaro. He rode from the old mine convinced of one thing: he'd have to risk returning by daylight so he could see into the interior. He stayed in the hills until he was past Trader Thorenson's place and made his way down and south to the big box elder. Dismounting, he laid out his bedroll started to undress when he heard the sound of horses approaching. He listened, his ear pressed to the ground and counted two horses. He was crouched, his hand on the big Colt at his hip, when the two horses came into dim sight. He took his hand from the Colt as he saw the moonlight glint on almost blond hair. He rose, Joseph's slightly rotund form taking shape on the other horse. His eyes met Millicent's as she reined to a halt. She wore a shirt hanging loose outside riding britches, unbuttoned at the neck for a arprising change, but her contained formality still held her me-lined face rigid. His eyes glowered at her.

"Joseph could've found his way here alone," he commented.

"I decided to help him," she returned tartly. "What'd you nd at the old mine?"

"Not much, but enough for another visit tomorrow," he aid, and told of the number of prints he'd found at the ntranceway. He turned his glance to Joseph.

"Everybody turned off, even my best places. Everybody raid," Joseph said.

"Afraid of what?" Fargo queried.

"Tarawa, Thunder Chief," Joseph said.

"No word on why he's been leaving every body naked?" argo pressed. "Or taking the wagons?"

Joseph shook his head. "Nothing, nobody talking."

"He trying to impress other tribes, maybe?" Fargo fered.

Joseph shrugged. "Maybe," he said. "One thing sure. e's got something big in the wind, and soon, Fargo, soon."

"Damn," Fargo swore as he frowned into the night. lillicent interrupted his thoughts.

"What about Thorenson and Mai-lin?" she asked.

He shook away thoughts about the Kiowa and focused on er. "With Willie Rank dead, and if Thorenson's our man, e has no more contact man. He'll have to send somebody to town to wait for whoever comes looking for Willie," argo said.

"We just watch whoever he sends, then," Millicent aswered.

"You sure as hell won't watch," Fargo said. "Not me, ther. If Thorenson sends one of his men he'll recognize . It won't take him long to smell a rat."

"Joseph?" Millicent suggested.

Fargo hesitated. He wanted Joseph to ride the hills some

more, perhaps to find something there. Joseph read hi
thoughts. "Not much chance, Fargo," he said. "Nobody lef
to ask."

"All right," Fargo said grimly. "You hang around at th
dance hall, Joseph. Wait and watch. If someone shows u
looking for Willie Rank, you'll see who moves to meet him
You get Millicent and she'll come here for me while you g
back and keep your eye on them." Fargo saw Millicent star
to protest, and he cut her off at once. "We'll all be waiting
just in different places," he said. "Meanwhile, come morn
ing, I'll have another look at that old mine."

"I start to hang around in dance hall tonight?" Josep
asked.

"Why not?" Fargo said.

Joseph's round face almost smiled. "Good. Need drink,
he remarked.

"I thought they wouldn't serve an Indian out here,
Millicent said.

"Half-breed, not Indian," Joseph said with a pride Farg
knew was all bitter mockery, but Millicent accepted
gravely. Joseph exchanged glances with Fargo and slowl
rode away. Millicent dismounted and walked to the edge
the longest branches of the spreading tree, her eyes movin
out over the hills touched by the pale silver of the hal
moon.

Fargo strolled over to stand beside her. "You stay to ki
me good night?" he asked blandly.

She whirled, brilliant blue eyes flashing. "Most certainl
not," she snapped. "I'm going to be cooped up in the hous
for a few days. I just want some fresh air before I go back.

"Suit yourself," Fargo said. "But I like my idea better."

"Is that all you ever think about?" Millicent asked wit
disapproval.

"Whenever I can," he said cheerfully, and watched as sh
gazed out over the hills again.

"This is a frightening land, frighteningly beautiful and frighteningly dangerous," Millicent said, looking at the man beside her. "Yet settlers keep coming, hoping. I don't understand them."

"They believe they can make it. They believe in themselves," he said.

"And are massacred for it," she said.

"Sometimes believing doesn't work out. Sometimes it does."

She cast an appraising glance at him. "What do you believe in, Fargo?" she asked.

"I believe in staying alive and staying happy," he told her.

"How do you do that out here?"

"Sleep light, shoot straight, and screw often." He laughed.

"A primitive philosophy," she sniffed disdainfully.

"Sometimes primitive is best," he said as she turned away and walked back to the dark-gray gelding. "You ought to try it sometime," he added.

She refused answering as she climbed into the saddle. "Good night," she said primly

" 'Night, Millie," he said.

"Millicent," she threw back as she rode away.

He laughed as he returned to his bedroll, undressed to shorts, and stretched out. He let himself sleep quickly and the warm night remained still until a purple martin woke him with its morning call. When he finished dressing, he rode up into the hills again. He stayed inside a stand of blue spruce till he was beyond the Thorenson ranch, and finally halted outside the old mine. He hid the Ovaro behind the protruding ledge to one side and hurried to the mine entranceway. Inside, the morning light sent yellow fingers of light down the main shaft. He walked cautiously along the tunnel, both sides of which were shored with wooden planking. He saw a kerosene lamp hanging from one wall, then another one farther into the shaft. A third lamp hung on the opposite wall where the light from the entranceway began to grow dim.

He examined the lamps and found they were all filled, no dust on any. They had been in recent use. He moved on farther down the main shaft and the light began to fade away. Ahead of him, the tunnel grew black and he spotted another lamp on the wall. He reached up and took it down, turned on low, and moved forward again. He continued along the main shaft until a second shaft joined it at right angles. A third shaft came in from the left a dozen yards further on, he saw, but he continued down the larger main shaft. The smell of damp dirt, a closed-in odor, drifted to his nostrils and he turned the lamp up as the blackness deepened. He'd gone on perhaps another dozen yards, he guessed, with the shaft narrowing until he had to duck his head. Suddenly it opened into a large, circular area. A rusted mine cart lay on its side near near the entrance to the area. He held the lamp high and let the light spread itself to the shored-up walls. A long pine table, chairs, and something else took shape. He let a slow whistle escape his lips. Six sets of chains and manacles were attached to the circular walls of the area and, to one side, a wire cage some six feet tall and four feet long.

He turned slowly, surveying the area. A seventh set of manacles and chains appeared at the other side of the round space. Fargo lowered the lamp. Any last uncertainty he had about Thorenson vanished. The man mined slave girls now, not silver. He'd added the sale of flesh to swindling, human degradation to double-dealing. Trader Thorenson had moved up and down the scale of dirtiness with ease. Fargo retreated up the mine shaft, taking care to replace and turn out the lamp just as he'd found it. The daylight came into sight as he moved up the shaft, and he halted as he reached the mine entrance. He peered outside, and satisfied he had

company, he pushed the boards open enough to slide
t. Casting another searching glance over the hillside, he
rried to where he'd hidden the Ovaro and sent the horse
gher into the hills before turning to cross on the high land.
He didn't head downward until he was certain he'd
ssed beyond Thorenson's ranch, and he slowly made his
y back to the big box elder. He dismounted and sat down
ainst the tree. He looked back and forth across the hills
yond and the flat land below, his discovery inside the old
ine clinging to him, a sour taste in his mouth. Evil came in
irs, the same yet so different. Thorenson and Tarawa.
e sprang from calculated, callous greed and absolute
morality, the other from a rage of towering savagery. But
e end result was the same: the complete disregard for
man life.

Fargo's gaze continued to scan the hills. The land grew
sh and ripe in the late-summer foliage while somewhere,
meplace, like an unseen, giant vulture, death waited,
thered itself. He could feel it, taste it. Not just the
essage Joseph had brought back, he grunted. The very air
still, the lush beauty a mask. A feeling of helplessness
rled inside him, frustrating, corroding. He leaned back
d let the day wear on, half-dozed in the warmth of the aft-
noon sun. He didn't expect any word from Millicent or
seph by day. A courier looking to contact Willie Rank
uld likely come by night, and Fargo relaxed as he
anned the land. The shadows had grown long when he
ught a movement at the top of the hill to his right. He sat
straight as a lone horseman appeared, his bronzed body
thed only in a loincloth.

The Indian peered down the hill and Fargo searched the
es that surrounded the brave with a slow, piercing gaze.
t nothing else moved, no other bronzed forms waited
hind him. The Indian seemed to be alone, and Fargo fol-
ved his gaze down the hill. He spotted the triangular pla-

toon flag first, and then the line of blue-clad troopers cam
into view, moving at a steady trot. He squinted and count
ten troopers, and he watched the soldiers ride straig
north until they disappeared from sight. He frowned as
glanced at the Indian, still motionless on the hill. The ca
tain didn't usually take his entire platoon out and he usual
patrolled in a wide circle, not in a straight line north. Pe
haps the captain had decided a change of tactics was
order, Fargo mused.

The Trailsman broke off thoughts as he saw the Indi
turn his pony and start to move away on the hill. "Damn
Fargo swore as he leapt to his feat and onto the Ovaro. T
Kiowa had been watching the platoon ride away, ar
satisfied, he had turned to go. Fargo spurred the Ovaro in
an uphill gallop. He wanted answers and maybe they we
in his grasp. He reached the top of the hill and sent t
Ovaro racing across the ridge, the Kiowa still in his sight.
he closed, he saw the Indian turn and catch sight of hi
coming out through the trees. Fargo swerved to cut acro
in front of the Indian, and the buck pulled his pony sharp
around to race off in the other direction. Fargo drew t
Colt as the Ovaro gained ground on the fleeing Kiowa. F
took aim, steadied his hand to keep his sight on the Indiar
bronzed shoulder. His finger started to press the trigg
when the buck swerved and raced down a narrow path o
of range.

Fargo lowered the Colt and sent the Ovaro down the pa
in time to see the buck swerve again to take another pa
sageway. Fargo stayed in pursuit and saw that despite h
twisting tactics, the Indian raced northward. With the ag
ity of his short-legged pony, the Kiowa swerved back ar
forth, making a careful shot impossible, and Fargo conce
trated on staying as close as he could. When the Kiov
reached the bottom of the hill, Fargo saw the river throu;
the trees and he sent the Ovaro into a full gallop. On

gain, he raised the Colt, tried to draw a bead on the Indian's shoulder, and once again held back. He needed to draw closer and he let the Ovaro close the distance with his longer, more powerful stride. The Kiowa reached the riverbank and turned his pony north upriver, racing along the edge of the river.

Fargo swung in behind him, close enough now, and he raised the Colt again, drew his sights on the redman's right shoulder blade. He fired, and at the same instant the Kiowa's pony jumped over a fallen tree trunk half on the bank and half in the water. Fargo saw his shot slam into the Indian's spine as the man rose up with his pony's leap, saw the Indian's back arch and split apart. The Indian screamed in pain as he toppled backward from his pony, his body landing on the fallen tree trunk. It hung there not unlike a piece of cloth tossed aside. Fargo halted and leapt to the ground, cursing with each step as he ran to the Kiowa. He lifted the Indian's head and stared at the lifeless eyes, which rolled back almost out of sight. He swore as he let the man's head fall back and turned away. But his eyes were narrowed in thought as he pulled himself onto the Ovaro and slowly rode away. Bad luck had called the shot. There'd be no answers, but perhaps it hadn't been a complete failure. Fargo stared at the river, the same river where the wagon tracks had disappeared. The Kiowa, racing to get away, had headed north. Because safety lay north, or because he was leading his pursuer away from something?

Fargo's eyes stayed narrowed in thought. Either way, the river held some kind of answer. The wagons had been rolled into the water, the tracks vanishing. But somewhere they had to have been rolled out again. And the tracks perhaps covered up, he grunted unhappily. But it was a lead of sorts—tenuous as it was—and when he returned to dismount beneath the big box elder, he had made a decision. He sat down as night swept over the land, chewed some

93

hardtack, and watched the night hours move with maddening slowness. He had stretched out on the cool grass a the half-moon rose into the midnight sky when he heard horse pounding the ground in a hard gallop. He was on hi feet, the Colt in his hand, as Millicent raced up.

"He's here. He came asking for Willie Rank, and one Thorenson's men came forward. Joseph slipped out and gc me. He's gone back to the dance hall," she said, words flun out breathlessly.

"How do you know it was one of Thorenson's men? Fargo asked as he vaulted onto the Ovaro.

"Joseph said he wore a brown leather vest," she said, an Fargo sent the Ovaro racing from beneath the tree.

"You get back to the house and stay there. I still want yo out of sight for now," he tossed at her. He touched th Ovaro's rump with a light tap, and the horse drove forwarc leaving the gray behind as though it were standing stil Fargo reached the edge of town and raced through Mai Street without slowing until he came into sight of the danc hall. He saw Joseph outside on his horse.

"They went off together, east, toward Thorenson place," Joseph said, and Fargo swung the Ovaro in a tigl circle and headed eastward with Joseph beside him. "Only few minutes ago. We can catch them." Fargo nodded an followed a pathway that led up a slow slope. The pat curved around a cluster of black oak, widened and flattene out. Joseph stayed beside him as he rode hard. Then th night suddenly split apart with a single, sharp explosion– the unmistakable sound of a six-gun.

Fargo reined up, an instant reaction, and cast a quic glance at Joseph. He knew dismay and frustration floode his face, and he saw Joseph nod solemn agreemen "Goddamn," Fargo swore as he sent the Ovaro forward. H came onto the lone figure lying motionless a few hundre

ards farther along the path, red slowly spilling from a
ingle hole in the man's temple.

"We go after the other one?" Joseph asked.

"No," Fargo answered bitterly. "Thorenson made the
ontact and had his man make sure there'd be no leaks.
Right now he still feels safe. He's got no reason to suspect
nybody's onto him. Let's keep it that way. It's our only
ard." He turned the Ovaro to head back the way they had
ome. "I'll stop by Millie's and tell her, or she'll come look-
ig for us," Fargo said.

"What now? More waiting?" Joseph asked.

"On this, not on the Kiowa," Fargo said tightly. Joseph
uestioned with silence. "They had to roll those wagons out
f the river someplace. We've got to find where. Come
orning, you go downriver; I'll head upriver. You find the
acks, see where they take you."

"How long we look?" Joseph asked.

"Give it two days. I can't see them floating the wagons for
onger than that," Fargo said as they reached Spineyleaf and
e drew up before the white frame house. Millicent opened
e door at once, held it open, and he motioned Joseph to
o with him as he dismounted and went inside. A lone lamp
ast a soft light in the living room and Fargo saw Mr. Soong
anding quietly to one side, almost a shadow figure. The
ld Chinese gentleman bowed his head and Fargo nodded
ack.

"I told Mr. Soong about Joseph Threehats helping you,"
Millicent said to Fargo. "What happened?"

Fargo told her of the gunshot that had ended the pursuit,
nd watched the dismay swim into her face.

"So we know nothing, really," she said.

"We know the contact was made and we know Thorenson
eals in slave girls," Fargo said, and quickly recounted what
e'd found inside the old mine.

"But we still don't know how or when Mai-lin is being brought in," Millicent said.

"Or *if* she is," Fargo remarked, and saw her eyes darken in a frown at once.

"What does that mean?" she questioned.

"You ever think that maybe somebody's plans changed and they sent her someplace else? Maybe he found a big buyer for her right off the boat. Thorenson may be getting a shipment of girls that won't include her," Fargo said.

Mr. Soong's voice came in softly. "The possibility has crossed my mind," he said.

"Good," Fargo grunted.

"There is a proverb from the Tao which says there is a time to assume the best of the worst. This is such a time," the old man answered.

"Maybe," Fargo agreed, and his eyes went to Millicent. "You stay out of sight till I get back," he told her.

"Get back from where?" She frowned.

"Joseph and I are going to try and find some wagon tracks," he said.

"What about Mai-lin?" Millicent protested.

"They just made the contact. I'd guess it'll be another few days before they make delivery," Fargo said.

"I don't guess anything. They could be bringing her in tomorrow," she countered.

"Possible," he conceded. "But not likely."

"You stay here and wait and see," Millicent demanded.

"No need to, and I can't afford to. The Kiowa aren't waiting. I figure I've two days to try to get a handle on whatever's in the wind. I'll be back then," he said. He ignored the accusations in her eyes as he walked from the house with Joseph, and he heard her slam the door shut as he rode away. He cast a glance at Joseph and saw the round face set with studied blandness. "Go on, say it, whatever you're thinking," he barked.

"Nothing going right," Joseph said. "Feel it inside. Big ouble all come together."

"Maybe not if we can find those damn wagon tracks," argo answered with more optimism than he felt. Joseph alted when they neared the box elder. "Two days," he runted, turned his sturdy-legged horse south, and rode f.

Fargo rode north past the big tree and headed for the dis- nt river. He halted to camp for the night before he ached it, slept quickly, and was in the saddle again as awn sent its pink-streaked fingers across the gray sky. He ached the river and turned north along the nearest bank. e set an easy riding pace, slow enough to let him scan the pposite bank as well, and he found himself stopping too ten to examine the soil wherever it took on a change in ppearance. Yet there was no other way, he knew, no way make time without the risk of missing a sign that was all ut obliterated, a print or a track that nature or the Kiowa ad changed.

The day wore on and the river deepened and grew wider. e wondered if Joseph were having any better luck. The verbank grew harder and the soil sandier as the river oved upland into the foothills of the Wind River Range. e continued to follow the water as the afternoon length- ned, then he decided to change tactics. He pulled the varo away from the riverbank and marked the spot by two hite birches that faced each other in exactly the same spot each bank. The Wind River Range foothills rose gently in ont of him, and his eyes searched the terrain as he rode. ogers had said Captain Schoonmaker operated out of two nall cabins at the base of the Wind River Range. Perhaps e captain had seen something that might help. It was orth the small diversion, Fargo mused, and he swung the into around as he finally spotted the two cabins side by de in front of a semi-circle of white fir. He sent the pinto

into a long-strided gallop and crossed the clear land to th
two cabins. The door of one hung open, but he saw no sig
of any sentry, not even an extra mount tied in back.

He felt the frown slide across his forehead as he di
mounted, his hand on the Colt. He used his foot to push th
door open wider. "Anybody home?" he called, and onl
silence answered. The Colt was in his hand as he steppe
inside the cabin. Two double-bunk beds, a table, and tw
chairs greeted him silently. An iron skillet rested again
the stones around a small fireplace. His gaze traversed th
room again. It was barren. Six clothing hooks on one wa
hung bare. No blankets, riding gear, extra boots, nothin
He backed out and tried the adjoining cabin. There wer
three double-bunk beds inside, but the rest of the cabin w
as bare as the other. Captain Schoonmaker had pulled ou
with his little platoon, it seemed. On orders or in flight
Fargo wondered.

He stepped outside and walked across the ground, eye
sweeping the soil. He saw the horseshoe prints of arm
horses and frowned down at the unshod prints of India
ponies.

He halted, his lips pursed in thought as he slowly let h
eyes scan the entire area outside the two cabins. Ther
were no signs of a battle, no blood on the ground, no broke
arrows or spent bullets, not even a wisp of torn clothin
But the outward signs could have been meticulousl
cleaned away. It wasn't likely, yet it was a possibility, and th
was a time of strange happenings. Eyes narrowed, he strod
to the fir trees that bordered the area and examined th
bark. He saw no places where bullets or arrows had tor
into the bark. A battle here would have certainly struc
some of the surrounding trees with signs to tell it had take
place, but there was nothing.

Fargo swung onto the Ovaro and headed back toward th
river. Whatever had happened, Captain Schoonmake

asn't on hand to give him any help. He rode slowly and
ay drifted into night. It was dark when he reached the
verbank and he decided to make camp beside the water.
eep was interrupted often as raccoons, martens, opos-
ms, and other night creatures came to the water to drink.
e knew the scurrying, scratching, and padding sounds of
ch, and he returned to sleep quickly each time. When
ay arrived, he washed in the river, dried himself, and
oved on northward again along the riverbank. The river
urved northeast along the base of the Wind River foothills.
rough an opening in the timber at his right he saw the
lling flatland stretching far into the distance. Fort Calder
as within a day's ride, and he discarded the idea of visiting
e fort and Major Armsted. He hadn't a day to waste on
hat would be a fruitless visit if Rogers were right about the
an.

He bent to his task of following the riverbank, but was
ustrated as he continued to find no signs of wagon tracks.
erhaps Joseph had done better, he hoped. Perhaps the
ne Kiowa had indeed fled north to pull him in the wrong
rection. He shook these thoughts away and concentrated
scanning the opposite bank when the river suddenly nar-
wed and curved sharply. Fargo followed the bank and
lfway around it when a stench struck him with almost
ysical force. The heavy flutter of huge, black wings filled
e air, and he felt a groan well up inside him as he sent the
varo forward around the rest of the curve. He halted and
ore into the silence.

He had found Captain Schoonmaker and his small pla-
on.

6

They looked like toy soldiers that had been broken an
thrown away—a small, blue-uniformed mound, decimate
by the sharp beaks of the vultures and riddled by arro
shafts. Fargo slowly moved forward along the riverbank an
his mouth thinned. The wagon tracks were still deep an
clear in the soft soil, coming up out of the river and rollin
up the bank and through a passage in the trees beyond. H
let his gaze sweep the scene again. Captain Schoonmak
and his pitifully small troop had come upon the wago
being pulled from the river. They had stumbled onto som
thing they were not supposed to see, and had paid the pri
for it. Their fate had been sealed that instant.

Fargo sighed deeply. The rest of what had happened fe
into place. The Kiowa had gone back to the twin cabins
be certain there were no others there who might ride out
sound alarm when the platoon failed to return. They'
found no one else, but had cleaned the cabins of everythin
that might be of use to them before riding away. Th
explained the double set of prints and no signs of a battle.

Tarawa, Thunder Chief, was cagey, wily, and thoroug
Fargo thought as he began to follow the wagon tracks, h

outh drawn tight. The tracks rolled northward at the edge
the white fir and he had followed for more than an hour
hen he picked up signs of more wagon tracks, not so deep
d older, the edges broken away. The afternoon sun
oved closer to the horizon and still the wagon tracks con-
ued through the wooded terrain. He counted six at least,
rhaps more. It had become hard to tell, for the wheels
lled single-file over one another's tracks, but he felt the
im excitement pulling at him. He'd followed for another
ur when he reined up sharply, the scent of campfire
oke drifting through the woods. The trees had grown
nser and the tracks circled their way through a narrow
th. Fargo followed, and the smell of the smoke grew
avier, took on added scents: meat being cooked, bear
ease, and fish oil.

He dismounted when the murmur of voices reached him,
d he moved forward on foot, leading the Ovaro behind
m. The sound grew louder and he halted to tether the
rse to a low branch. He dropped to a crouch and went on,
es sweeping the trees, but he found no sentries posted.
e Kiowa felt securely hidden away, and with good reason.
e camp, when he came in sight of it through the trees,
as a large, cleared area surrounded by firs and balsams,
d he moved forward at a crawl to halt a half-dozen yards
om the edge of the trees. Four tepees lined one side,
ree-pole Kiowa tepees, and a pair of campfires at each end
the clearing were hung with rabbit being roasted. The
mp itself was crowded, mostly braves but several children
d squaws. It might have been a typical Indian camp were
not for the riveting sight along the one side.

Eight wagons, Conestogas, two without canvas, their
re bows curving across the tops of the frame. A dozen
dians were climbing into the wagons, carefully taking
eir places; they were all wearing trousers, shirts, and
ts, the squaws dresses and bonnets, and children in their

own children's outfits. Three of the women wore long blo[nd]
hair, as did two of the children. Even close as he was, th[ey]
looked exactly as though they were settlers, the scalp-wi[gs]
on the women hanging down long enough to be clearly vi[si]
ble. A Kiowa wearing a plaid shirt and trousers took t[he]
reins of his wagon, a blue-bonneted woman beside him.

Fargo's eyes went to the man that strode into view,
naked except for a loincloth, tall, muscled, bronzed bo[dy]
glistening with bear grease. He turned and Fargo saw [a]
strong face, a stern, merciless face that seemed to stare [as]
the eagle stares, piercing, penetrating, commandin[g.]
"Tarawa, Thunder Chief," Fargo breathed aloud. The m[an]
strode back and forth along the wagons, making commen[ts]
in short, terse clusters, and Fargo saw some of those on t[he]
wagons adjust their clothes, pull the scalp wigs down mor[e.]
Tarawa barked again and those in the wagons rose a[nd]
dropped to the ground. They stood aside as they pulled [off]
their white man's clothing and another group of Kio[wa]
began to dress in the outfits. They climbed onto the wago[ns]
and took their places, the men, the bewigged squaws, a[nd]
the children with their scalp-wigs. Once again, Tara[wa]
strode back and forth along the wagons, stepped bac[k,]
peered, barked orders, and surveyed the sight.

"A dress rehearsal," Fargo murmured aloud. "He's ho[ld]
ing a goddamn dress rehearsal." Fargo rested on one kn[ee]
as he watched, and he felt amazement, anger, and star[k,]
searing realization curdle inside him. Tarawa's bronze[d,]
muscled figure moved to one of the wagons and lifted t[wo]
children down to the ground. He pulled their scalp-wi[gs]
from them as they shed clothes, and he called two oth[er]
Kiowa children and had them put on the wigs and cloth[es.]
He boosted them onto the wagon and stepped back. Appa[r]
ently satisfied with the changes he'd made, he moved alo[ng]
the line of wagons, his piercing eyes taking in ea[ch]
masquerading figure. He paused at one of the wagon[s,]

102

justed the hat and bonnet on two of the Indians, and
oved on, halting and barking commands. Unlike so many
the other tribes who shared the Siouan or Algonquian
language, the Kiowa spoke their own Kiowan tongue, and
argo understood only a little of it. But he caught the Thun-
r Chief's words that said "more tomorrow, when others
me."

Fargo watched as the Indians climbed down from the
agons, took off clothing, and put the garments into the
onestogas. The squaws returned to tending the fires and
e men sat down in clusters in the last light of the day. But
e unexplained was suddenly explained: the naked bodies,
ipped of every stitch of clothing; the scalped children and
omen; the wagons spirited away with such great care to
ave no trail that could lead others to the truth. All was now
arningly clear, laid out before him, all part of a plan fash-
ned with diabolic cleverness and carried out with savage
scipline. But the explanations paled beside the Kiowa
ief's goal, and Fargo leaned against an oak as the magni-
de of it swept over him.

Tarawa prepared to attack Fort Calder, with a cleverness
d a daring that ensured success. The fort had resisted pre-
ous attacks and the Kiowa chief knew that to win he had to
t inside the fort with enough men to keep the gates open.
ith the gates open, his warriors could sweep inside and
erwhelm the defenders. And he had devised the way, its
ry simplicity the key to its success. The fort's gates would
y open in welcome for the approaching wagon train. The
ldiers standing guard would see only one more caravan of
oneers arriving to resupply at the fort. They would catch
e glint of the sun on the long hair of a little girl and see the
nd blow the tresses of the women from beneath their
wered bonnets.

They'd not see the masquerade until the lead wagons
re inside the fort, the others passing through the gates. It

would be too late then. The wagons would erupt, sava
surprise among their weapons, Tarawa more than willing
sacrifice those lead attackers. By the time the defende
pulled themselves together, his warriors would be racing
the attack, sweeping inside the fort while the first of his w
riors had wedged their wagons against the gates to ke
them open.

Fargo cursed silently. He was indulging in no idle spec
lation. He foresaw the terrible reality that only waited
become fact. The Kiowa began to gather around the tv
campfires as dark fell, and Fargo watched with his eyes na
rowed in thought. Tarawa wasn't ready to put his gre
deception into action yet. He had spoken of more warrio
arriving tomorrow and more dress rehearsals. He had tv
perhaps three days' time, Fargo figured as he rose to l
feet. He began to back away from the Kiowa camp, turni
to creep silently to where he'd left the Ovaro. Climbi
onto the horse, he retreated carefully, stealthily, throu
the woodland as he let plans begin to take shape in l
mind. He had to get back to Spineyleaf, to the captain a
his handful of troopers: no force with which to engage t
Kiowa in head-on combat, but he'd show the captain how
borrow a page from the Indian's notebook of tactics a
swoop down, strike and run, vanish and reappear to hit a
run again.

The maneuver would be enough to make Tarawa reali
his plan had been uncovered. The Kiowa chief would p
back with his masquerade for massacre. He'd realize at on
that the attack meant that the fort may have been alert
and be ready and waiting. The Kiowa would have to hold
on his plans. He had shown himself too clever and careful
risk his entire force being cut down. The vital thing was
make the Kiowa hold off, think twice, and use the time
send a rider to the fort. Fargo pushed away further thoug
and bent to racing the Ovaro through the woodland and o

to the moonlit slopes. He rode hard, the Ovaro's power-
l stride devouring distance. Without the need to follow
e riverbank's curving path, he cut straight across the land
d halted only when daybreak and exhaustion came
gether. He pulled the Ovaro into a dense stand of haw-
orns and slid from the saddle to curl up on the ground. He
ept instantly, allowed himself four hours, and was riding
rough the tall brush again before the sun had climbed into
e noon sky. He took care not to drive the horse too hard,
l too aware that there'd be little chance to rest when he
ached Spineyleaf.

The day had slid into afternoon when the town came into
ew, the long barracks building marking the north end of
wn. Fargo slowed the Ovaro's gallop as he reached the
arracks and a frown dug at his brow. The door hung open,
e barracks empty, silent, only a broken stirrup lying on
e floor. Fargo spurred the pinto on again and galloped
to town to rein up before the blacksmith's shop. "You see
e army ride out?" he called to the smith.

"Couple of days ago," the man answered. "Ordered back
Fort Calder, I heard."

Fargo nodded and his heart sank. That was what the lone
iowa scout had watched, the platoon pulling out. He can-
red across town to the small white house and dismounted
Millicent rushed out, a blue blouse accenting the bril-
ance of her azure eyes, which were filled with urgency.
oseph show yet?" Fargo asked.

"No," she said, and his lips tightened in disappointment
ut not surprise. Joseph wouldn't have ridden back full tilt.
Mai-lin is here," Millicent said, and he eyed her sharply.

"How do you know that?" Fargo asked.

"I ran into Thorenson, at the general store," she
answered. "He was getting into a buckboard. The Mongo-
an, Kwang, was with him. I had to tell him I was staying

105

here. He obviously was wondering what I was doing in town."

"Damn," Fargo bit out.

"What do we do now?" Millicent questioned.

"You keep low until I get back," he said.

"Get back?" She frowned, instant protest leaping into her eyes. "You're not going anywhere now. We've got to get Mai-lin."

"He has to wait for his buyers. She'll be safe till then," Fargo said.

"Safe? In that brute's hands, maybe beaten every day or heaven knows what else?" Millicent returned.

"No. You want to sell a yearling for a fancy price she's got to be in good condition," Fargo said. "I'll be back. I've got to find a way to stop a massacre."

"A massacre?" She frowned.

"Tarawa is going to hit Fort Calder. He's set up a plan that'll work," Fargo said. "There are a hundred people inside that fort, men, women, kids. He'll kill every living soul there and then burn the fort to the ground. I've got to try to stop that."

"You can't. There's no way," Millicent said.

"Maybe not, but I've got to try," Fargo said. "Goddamn, I've got to try."

"No, you're staying here, to save Mai-lin. Maybe you won't get back, maybe anything. Mai-lin comes first," Millicent flung back.

"I told you, there's time, she has time yet," Fargo said.

"You don't know that. You can't be sure," she returned.

"Sure enough. But a hundred people will be massacred in another day," Fargo said.

"I paid you to save Mai-lin. That comes first," Millicent said angrily.

"A hundred people come first. A hundred lives against one," he told her.

She glared at him, the brilliant blue eyes flashing fury. "You made a contract," she said.

"I made one with myself a long time ago," Fargo growled. "I'll be back."

"No, dammit, don't you dare leave," she half-screamed.

"Go to hell, Millicent," he said.

She stopped, surprise flashing in her face. "That's the first time you've called me Millicent," she said.

"Decided it fits right. Millie is soft, warm, caring. Millicent is cold, stiff, selfish. You're Millicent, all right," he said.

"I'm not selfish. Mai-lin is a person, a friend, someone I've been close to for three years. She's not somebody on a wagon train somewhere. I can't feel any other way. Can't you understand that?" Millicent retorted, and he saw her eyes grow misty.

"Maybe you can't," Fargo conceded. "But I can't feel differently, either. A hundred lives against one. I can't balance it off." He turned, swung himself onto the Ovaro, and looked down at her. She stood with hands made into fists, held rigidly at her sides, despair and anger mixed together in her eyes. "Joseph comes, tell him to ride fast and follow the river north," Fargo said. He turned the Ovaro and rode away at a fast trot.

She was still standing outside the small white house, he saw as he rode out of town. He set the Ovaro in a steady pace back the way he'd come, cutting away time by moving along the flat land and turning into the hills later. The day faded into night and he kept on until he felt the pinto tiring, his steps growing heavy, the long stride shortening. He halted, unsaddled the horse, and used the saddle to rest his back against as he lay down and slept, his own body drinking in slumber.

He woke before daylight and set off again, forcing himself to slow his pace as the morning came and let him see the

Wind River Range in the distance. But the Ovaro was showing fatigue. He'd been driven at a pace that would've done in most horses. Fargo slowed and cursed at the circumstances that had made him drive his horse so unmercifully. He ran his hand down the warm, smooth hide of the powerful black neck, soothing, letting touch speak. He steered the horse up into the timber of the foothills, let the Ovaro set his pace upward. The afternoon sun hung high in the sky when he reached the heavy woodland of the Wind River Mountains and traced his way back to the Kiowa camp, his eyes peering through the sun-flecked forest.

A herd of white-tailed deer scurried away to his right, and a little distance on, a covey of ruffed grouse took wing in their almost vertical flight, but he saw nothing else to make him take cover. The Kiowa felt secure in their woodland camp. He picked up the wagon tracks he had first followed from the riverbank. He moved slowly, the Ovaro pulling himself forward on tired, strained legs, and Fargo dismounted as soon as he caught the campfire odor. He led the Ovaro on foot as he drew close to the camp, halted, draped the horse's reins loosely over a low branch, and went forward alone.

The Kiowa camp came into sight through the trees and Fargo cropped to a low crouch as he made his way to a cluster of tall pine brush that gave him a view of the entire camp. A line of clothed figures occupied four of the wagons and Tarawa was still giving instructions, Fargo saw. As he watched, most of the figures climbed down from the wagon and two others climbed onto the driver's seat of one Conestoga. One buck, clothed in plaid shirt, trousers boots, and a flat-brimmed hat, picked up the reins as though driving. The other disguised brave sat beside him. Tarawa barked instructions and the man holding the reins shifted to hunch forward in a position more typical of a man who had driven long and hard. The Kiowa chief nodded ttered crisp comments, and the two men stepped from the wagon as Tarawa allowed another nod of approval.

The bastard, Fargo swore silently. The chief was making sure that every detail of his masquerade of death was perfect, and Fargo watched as the Kiowa chief dismissed the others who quickly, with distaste, pulled clothes off and put them into the wagons. While the braves and squaws returned to camp duties, Tarawa sat down and stared into the woods to his left, his face severe, frowning, black eyes piercing. The Indian sat immobile, as if carved in bronze, and Fargo saw the campfires burn higher as the afternoon began to slide into dusk. Purple-gray filtered into the woods when Fargo saw the Kiowa chief suddenly rise to his feet, a single, effortless motion, his body unfolding into tallness.

Fargo followed the Indian's gaze and saw the figures taking shape among the trees, horses and riders materializing ghostlike. A shout of welcome broke out as the riders came into the camp. They rode slowly, majestically, lining up in front of Tarawa, and Fargo counted forty braves. As Tarawa greeted the new arrivals, Fargo let his eyes move over the camp, a rough series of calculations falling into place in his mind. The Kiowa chief had to commit some sixty of his force to the wagons. Half would be disguised warriors, the rest disguised squaws and children. That would give him thirty braves inside the fort to launch the attack while the squaws wedged the gates open with the wagons. Fargo's glance swept the camp again and got a quick count of forty braves besides those that had just arrived. He swore under his breath. It was a force more than enough to do the job, especially given the two major weapons they would have: surprise and overwhelming savagery.

The new arrivals dismounted and sat down, and Fargo's attention returned to the scene before him. The squaws brought food to the newcomers, and Tarawa rose to address the camp. A respectful silence fell at once. Fargo grimaced

at his inability to understand much of the Kiowan, b
Tarawa believed in emphasizing his points and he accom
panied his words with gestures.

One unmistakable fact came through his exhortations a
he used a kind of sign language as he spoke. The wago
would roll out with the dawn, Tarawa said, the plan t
destroy Fort Calder begin. Fargo felt his mouth turn into
thin slash across his face as the Kiowa finished to shouts o
approval. Tarawa strode into the largest of the tepees an
Fargo watched the others put out fires and begin to settl
down for the night.

He stared across the camp to the line of Conestoga wag
ons across from where he crouched, and felt helpless. H
couldn't wait for Joseph. There was every chance Josep
hadn't returned to Spineyleaf yet. Even if he had and if he
gotten the message from Millicent, he'd not reach the track
in the riverbank till late in the day. But the Kiowa had to b
stopped before those wagons rolled through the open gate
of the fort. He thought of riding hell-bent-for-leathe
through the night and day to reach Fort Calder, but th
thought died quickly. The Ovaro was an exhausted horse
He'd been pushed hard for three days. He needed at least
full day's rest to stand up under the kind of riding it'd take t
reach Fort Calder in time. If the Ovaro went lame, it'd b
all over. There'd be no chance to warn the fort or to find
way to disrupt the Kiowa's plan. But somehow, someway
he had to do just that. Somehow, someway, he had to ri
away the masquerade for massacre before it was too late.

Fargo cursed softly. He'd no damn idea how he could d
that without being riddled through with Kiowa arrows, an
the feeling of helplessness grew stronger. But one fac
burned with searing clarity. If there was a way, a faint glim
mer of hope of succeeding, he had to stay with the Kiowa
Yet that, too, seemed an impossible task. Following alon
behind them was out of the question. The wagon trai

would roll onto flat, open land soon enough, come the day. The main Kiowa force would stay far behind the wagons. But he couldn't follow without going out onto the open plains, where he'd be spotted at once. He'd have to find a way to go along with the wagons, to become part of the wagon train.

But how, dammit? he asked himself. Trying to take a place as one of the masqueraders was certain death. He'd be uncovered damn quickly if not at once. Again, he swore in helpless anger as he scanned the wagons. The undercarriage of the big Conestogas offered no place to cling to, but suddenly his gaze came to a halt at the last wagon in line. It was not a Conestoga, but a canvas-covered chuck wagon. Carawa had taken a chuck wagon to give his wagon train that last touch of complete authenticity. Fargo's eyes focused at the underside of the chuck wagon, at the sling suspended there. Made of cowhide, the sling was a part of every chuck wagon. Called a possum belly, the cowhide sling was the place the cook stored the fuel he collected along the way for his fires, whether it was wood or buffalo chips.

The possum belly was strong, deep enough and long enough, and Fargo felt a spiral of excitement rise up inside him. The Indians had examined every one of the wagons long ago. They'd have no reason to do it again. It was his one chance to stay with the wagon train; he had to take it, despite the certainty of instant death if he were discovered. He leaned his back against a tree as the Indian encampment grew quiet, and he closed his eyes and let himself sleep. His body responded with exhausted gratitude.

The night was deep into the hanging hour just before dawn when he woke; in a low crouch, he began to circle his way to the wagons. He moved slowly, testing his way each step. A snapped twig would sound loud as a six-gun in the silence. The first streaks of day had begun to edge their way along the sky when he came to the wagons. He went down

111

on his belly and began to crawl toward the chuck wagon. Kiowa warriors slept in clusters only a few feet from the wagons, and he snaked his way forward until he reached the possum belly. He rose to one knee and ran his hands along the wide, hanging piece of cowhide, pulling and testing to make sure it hung securely. Moving slowly, he drew one leg up and slid his big frame into the cowhide sling. He disappeared inside it at once, and it swayed for an instant. He lifted his head and saw he was able to see out. Satisfied, he pulled back inside the cowhide sling and managed to stretch his legs. The possum belly wasn't at all uncomfortable, not unlike resting in a hammock. He lay for another hour and then heard the sounds of the camp waking. He fought down the urge to peer over the cowhide sling; he didn't dare, not with squaws and kids waking, bending over, climbing into wagons. He needed only one pair of quick eyes to see him and it was all over.

Fargo lay still, but he knew what took place as surely as if he'd peered out. His ears were trained to see when the eyes didn't dare to look. He knew the Kiowa were putting on the white man's clothes as he heard the rustle of garments and the voices raised in excitement. Tarawa moved up and down the camp, barking orders, his voice growing close and then receding. Fargo felt the wagon shake. They were hitching the horses, and soon after, he heard the creak of the big Conestogas as they began to roll. Finally the chuck wagon pulled out and swung in at the end of the line. The wagon moved slowly downhill and Fargo listened to the sound of Indian ponies riding along with the wagons. The braves stayed with the wagons as the big wheels bumped their way downhill. But the possum belly swung in a smooth rhythm, and if he closed his eyes, he could imagine he was in a hammock somewhere, only the occasional jounce of the wagon to dispel the illusion.

He felt the wagon level out finally. They had reached the

t land and the Indian ponies cantered away. Fargo waited
l the sound of their hooves faded into the distance before
 pushed himself up enough to peer over the edge of the
whide sling. He saw the line of Conestogas stretched
ead as he peered out through the wheels of the chuck
gon. Prairie stretched out on all sides, and a few dozen
rds to the rear he saw Tarawa and his warriors following at
low, casual pace. But the Kiowa chief's stern, penetrating
re had lost none of its commanding presence, he noted,
e Indian riding straight, regally, his bronzed body shining
the sun.

Fargo lay back in his cowhide pouch and let plans begin
 take shape in his mind. Joseph would find the empty
dian camp and the Ovaro nearby. He'd be quick to sur-
se some of what had happened. He'd take the Ovaro, fol-
w the tracks of the wagons and Tarawa's warriors, and
ece together the rest. But there was little chance he'd
tch up in time. He'd have to stay clear of Tarawa and his
rriors, and on the open plain that meant hanging far back
 making a very wide circle. Help from Joseph was almost a
rtain impossibility, Fargo realized. Whatever had to be
ne, he'd have to do it alone. It was really simple enough.
e had few choices. He had to wait, stay undiscovered until
e wagon train neared the fort. His was the last wagon in
e. When the fort came into sight, he'd crawl from his hid-
g place, cut down the Kiowa driving, unhitch one of the
rses, and race like hell for the fort.

He managed to summon a grim smile. They couldn't fire
 him without giving themselves away. They'd be caught
 in their own deception. He stretched in the sling,
joying the thought. The wagons rolled slowly onward and
e sling swayed soothingly. He let himself half-doze,
lled himself up to peer out regularly. At one point the
d wagons curved to go around a sinkhole, and he had a
g look at the figures riding the wagons. Their disguises

were damn near perfect, even as close as he was; he swo
bitterly and retreated into the sling again. When he rose
peer out the next time, he saw that Tarawa's warriors ha
dropped back out of sight. He scanned the horizon li
ahead at once. The fort was still not in sight, but the Kio
chief was taking no chances. Fargo stayed up on one elb
and watched the wagons in front of him roll onward, but I
finally settled down again when the fort failed to come in
sight across the seemingly unending prairie.

He lay waiting and felt the afternoon sun move towa
the horizon, the rays coming in under the wagon from t
side. Perhaps another hour had gone by when he sudden
felt the wagon begin to pick up speed. He immediately ro
to peer over the top of the sling, and saw the square bulk
Fort Calder in the distance. He saw something else, and I
out an oath. Tarawa and his main force had come into sig
again, still far back but closing distance. Fargo felt t
chuck wagon gather more speed; the lead Conestoga set t
pace, the horses pulling hard. Another quick glance ba
showed Tarawa still gaining.

"Son of a bitch," Fargo swore aloud. The Kiowa chief h
arranged to put on a fake attack, another stroke of his da
diabolic cleverness. Those watching from the fort would I
sure to open the gates wide for the fleeing wagon trai
They might even send out a squad to engage the pursui
warriors, draining the fort of fighting men inside.

The chuck wagon raced full out now and Fargo clung
the sides of the cowhide sling as it swayed and bounced. I
cursed again in frustration. Tarawa's maneuver ha
destroyed his own plan, too. There was no time left
unhitch one of the horses and race ahead to the fort. But I
had to do something to rip away the deception. He could
stay in the sling and watch the Kiowa's plans go off withou
hitch. He pulled himself up over the edge of the wild
swaying sling, clung to one side as he flipped himself o

s feet hit the ground and he felt pain shoot up his legs as
clung to the sling and let himself be dragged under the
gon. He shot an arm out as the wagon bounced him side-
ys, and he curled his hand around the bottom edge of the
me. He let go of the sling with his other hand and pulled
nself up onto the side of the wagon, his feet dragging
ngside. The canvas-covered stake sides were within
ch; he caught hold of one, felt his shoulder and arm
scles cry out in protest as he pulled himself up to the top
the frame. The canvas fell inward as he pushed himself
o the wagon. The Indian driving was busy holding the
ns, his ten-gallon hat pulled low over his face. He never
ard the big man come up behind him from inside the
gon until the blow sent him flying over the edge of the
t.

Fargo seized the reins as he climbed onto the seat. The
t was close enough for him to see the sentries atop the
oden wall waving on the racing wagon train. Tarawa, he
v, stayed just far enough behind to make the picture per-
t. The two lead wagons were perilously close to reaching
open gates, and Fargo saw the squad of blue-clad troop-
sweep out from the fort, racing at an angle to meet
rawa's pursuing warriors.

'No, goddammit," Fargo shouted into the wind. The
wa chief was going to win, after all. He'd set it up too
rfectly, planned it all too well. Fargo snapped the reins
rd and swung the chuck wagon out of line. Lighter than
heavy Conestogas, he raced past the nearest wagon,
ne abreast of the next to last in line. He pulled the chuck
gon out in a half-circle, flung a glance at the fort. The first
nestoga was racing through the open doors and Fargo
rsed as he swung the chuck wagon in, raced it broadside
the nearest Conestoga. He swung at the last moment,
dded the wagon broadside to smash it hard into the
nestoga. He leapt from the seat as the Conestoga went

over on its side with the chuck wagon, axles snapping a
wheels splintering off. But those on the wagon we
sprawling, hats and scalp-wigs flying into the air.

Fargo saw the sentries atop the fort pointing, othe
rushing up to see. The masquerade was done wit
exposed, but the Kiowa in the wagons still racing for the fo
were quick to realize what had happened. They react
with the speed and fury of inborn instinct. Bows and arro
and a few rifles appeared as they mounted a barrage of fi
On one knee, Fargo saw three of the troopers rushing pa
go down, and his eyes went to the fort. The first tv
Conestogas were halted against the gates, holding the
open, and the Kiowa, squaws fighting beside the brave
poured arrows into those trying to reach the gates fro
inside. The other four Conestogas were still racing towa
the fort, and Fargo rose, saw a riderless army mount halt
nearby, and ran to the horse. He vaulted into the saddle a
sent the horse at a full gallop toward the open gates. T
Kiowa had their backs to him, intent on fighting off tl
troopers trying to reach the wagons from inside the fo
Fargo raised the Colt as he raced at the gates and fired a ve
ley at the nearest wagon, swinging the gun in a short arc
he fired. Six figures toppled from the wagon, and he thre
himself low over the horse's withers as the Kiowa in tl
other wagon turned to send a shower of arrows his way. Tl
shafts passed over his head as he raced the horse throug
the gates, still bent low in the saddle. He reached ou
seized the cheekstraps of the nearest horse, and the anim
came forward with him, the wagon rolling away from tl
gate.

He let the wagon roll on as he leapt from the army mour
scooped up a rifle on the ground, and joined a half-doze
troopers pouring fire into the other wagon. Return fire fro
the other wagon fell silent and two troopers seized tl
horses by the loose reins and pulled the wagon away fro

gate. Others rushed up to help swing the gates shut, the
t of the remaining wagons less than a few feet away.
·go heard the arrows slam into the gates as the wagons
ng by, and he turned to let his glance take in the com-
nd. Other wagons, brought in earlier for supplies, were
inst one wall and he saw men and women huddled in fear
h their children. Troopers climbed to the top of the wall
l he raced up a flight of wooden steps to join them, the
y rifle still in his hand. The Kiowa had circled their
aining wagons and were racing away, but Fargo's eyes
ved out to where Tarawa's warriors pursued the last of
: troopers that had sped outside, and he groaned
·ardly at the blue-clad forms that littered the ground.

Ie turned away and noticed a trickle of blood down his
:arm where a Kiowa shaft had scraped the skin. He
nbed down the steps as he saw a man stride from the bar-
ks toward him, the insignia on his uniform marking him
Major Armsted. The short-cropped hair and the both
nd and bitter face of the man beside him was instantly
iliar. Fargo's eyes met Captain Rogers' grave stare. "It
alls in place now, doesn't it?" the captain said, and Fargo
lded. "They'd have all made it in if it hadn't been for
,," the captain added.

·argo's nod held no pride in it. The massacre had been
haps only delayed. Tarawa had no bloody victory, but
d wiped out a good part of the fort's defenders. His eyes
nt to Major Armsted and took in a small-boned face, a
all chin, and a hairline mustache over a thin, tight
uth. "You're Fargo. Captain Rogers told me about your
uting for him," the man said. "We can hold out now."

I hope so, because Tarawa's not finished trying," Fargo
l.

he man's eyes searched his face for understanding,
·go saw. "I thought they'd take off when I sent the squad

117

out. They usually do when they're just chasing a wag
train," the major said.

"That's what they expected you'd think." Fargo nodd
"I won't fault you for that. I will for everything else."

The major tried to draw authority around himself at on
"I won't take that from a civilian, Fargo," the man said.

"Take it from Schoonmaker and his men. You can cal
their comments from the grave," Fargo said, and watch
the man's small-boned face drain of color.

"Goddamn," Captain Rogers breathed. "Ah, hell."

Fargo glanced skyward. "Be dark in fifteen minutes,"
said. "You'd best get your fort ready for the morning."

"We can hold them off," Major Armsted said. "We alw.
have."

Fargo fixed the man with a hard stare. "You trying to c
vince yourself?" he barked. "You've lost half your troo
and that Kiowa chief out there knows it. He's got enou
men to hit hard, and he's going to do it."

"I've told Captain Rogers to press all the men from
wagon trains in here into service," the major answer
"This fort will stand." He spun on his heel and walk
briskly toward his office beside the barracks building.

"Armsted's monument," Captain Rogers said to Far
his voice tight with bitterness. "Maybe he's right. May
we can hold."

"Not this time. He's lost too much firepower to keep
Kiowa off, even using the settlers," Fargo said.

"Don't see that we've much choice but to stay and figh
the captain said.

"Maybe not," Fargo said. "I'm going to get some sle
first, then I'll think on it."

The captain started to walk away and paused. "Thanks
trying," he said.

"Trying doesn't count. Winning does," Fargo said.
captain walked on to organize the defenses, and Fargo w.

118

ed to the stables in a corner of the fort. He found a spot
ere the hay made a good soft bed, and lay down. An
aausted body didn't work at its best. Neither did a weary
ad. He let himself sleep at once and shut out the sounds
m outside.

Ie slept hard but woke himself when the new day pre-
ed to appear, the last of the night still lingering. He
ished the hay from his clothes, paused at a water keg to
sh and refresh himself, and climbed the steps to the top
the wall. Captain Rogers and a dozen soldiers manned
front wall. The two side walls were lined with a combi-
ion of troopers and settlers from the wagons inside the
t. Fargo's eyes traveled across the line of backup troops
ting below the top of the wall, below the line of fire,
dy to fill in for anyone hit.

The gray dawn pushed night away and he turned to peer
oss the prairie. Tarawa and his warriors were gathered in
distance, but Fargo's eyes halted on the single horse-
n far at the other side, leading a riderless Ovaro.
amn," he said, grinning as he saw Joseph break into a full
lop as the darkness lifted, holding the Ovaro close beside
1. "Open the gates. Let that man in," Fargo shouted.
"Do as he says," Captain Rogers called down, and Fargo
v the soldiers at the gates slide the big bolt back to pull
gates open.

Fargo's glance returned to where Joseph raced for the
t. It was easy enough to piece together what had hap-
ned. Joseph had followed the tracks and reached the
ne in the night. He'd stayed back to wait the dawn when
ose at the fort could see him clearly. As he watched,
rgo saw Tarawa send out a half-dozen braves to cut off the
er streaking for the fort. But Joseph had too much dis-
ce on them already and the Indians turned away as they
v the task was futile.

119

Fargo climbed down from the wall as Joseph raced t[o]
halt inside the fort and the gates were slammed shut aga[in].

"Brought your horse, Fargo," Joseph remarked.

"Thanks," Fargo said with the same blandness.

"Plenty dead outside," Joseph commented.

"He almost pulled it off," Fargo said.

"That lady plenty mad at you, Fargo," Joseph sa[id].
"Almost didn't tell me. I keep asking."

"She can be real bitchy, all right," Fargo said.

"She said I should stay help her."

"What'd you say?"

"I laugh. She get mad again."

A shout cut off further exchanges. "Here they come," [one]
of the troopers on the wall called down.

Fargo yanked the big Sharps from the saddle holster [on]
the Ovaro and charged up the steps; Joseph followed w[ith]
his own rifle. Tarawa had sent his forces in two groups, [one]
attacking from the right, the other from the left. Fargo t[ook]
up a spot near the corner of the wall, held his fire as the oth-
ers began to shoot. When he had a charging Kiowa wel[l in]
his sights, he pressed the trigger and the Indian flew fr[om]
his pony as though he'd been atop a bucking bronco.

But the Kiowa came in with a style of attack that was b[oth]
disciplined and effective. Tarawa had them wheel, fire th[eir]
arrows in clusters at one area, and race out of range, tu[rn]
and come in for another clustered volley. "Damn the cle[ver]
bastard," Fargo muttered. After a volley of arrows, Fa[rgo]
followed a retreating Indian with his sights, fired, a[nd]
watched the buck sprawl forward over his pony and fal[l to]
the ground. Tarawa allowed six of the flying, clustered s[or]-
ties and then withdrew, and Fargo stepped back from [the]
wall, his eyes on Captain Rogers.

"How many?" he heard the captain ask a corporal.

"Four dead, three wounded," the soldier said.

Fargo saw Major Armsted climb the steps to the to[p]

he wall. The man met his hard gaze with his small-boned
ace twitching nervously.

"Four now, five or six maybe at the next attack," Fargo
aid. "He'll keep whittling you down."

"He's paying, too," the major said.

"Not enough," Fargo snapped.

"Here they come again," a soldier called, and Fargo
eturned to the wall. This time Tarawa sent the entire force
a until they came within firing range, then they peeled off
ato three groups. But again, they fired volleys of arrows.
Iost missed, but like shotgun pellets, enough landed. It
lso allowed them to fire more quickly without waiting to
ngle out a target. Fargo found he had to duck with every-
ne near him as a clustered volley of arrows came his way.
Vhen he rose to fire back, the attackers were racing out of
ange. Tarawa broke off the attack after another half-dozen
orties, and Fargo glanced down the wall. He counted four
feless forms, two of them from the wagons below.

"Five dead, two wounded," the corporal called, and
argo met Major Armsted's nervous glance.

"He's whittling pretty damn well," Fargo said.

"Why doesn't he just mount a full attack?" the major
most whined.

"Why should he, when he can keep cutting you down?"
argo answered. "When you've lost more men, he'll attack.
ire arrows, I'd guess. He'll cover the front wall with them
ad you won't have enough firepower left to stop him. He'll
arn the wall down and sweep in to finish the job."

"There's nothing we can do," the major said.

"Don't fight back," Fargo barked, and saw the man
own, his jaw dropping open. Captain Rogers blinked in
arprise, also. "Keep everybody down except a man in the
arner post. Let Tarawa fire his arrow clusters. Nobody
ays up to shoot back and nobody gets hit. You don't lose
ay more men that way," Fargo said.

"And Tarawa?" the major asked.

"He'll realize he's wasting arrows. He'll see that he has t[o] make his move against us as we stand, no more whittlin[g] away men," Fargo said.

Major Armsted wrestled with the thought, his lips com[ing] together to make his small mouth smaller. "Pass th[e] word, Captain," he said to Rogers. "Everybody stays dow[n] except one man to keep watch."

Major Armsted moved away as the captain hurried off t[o] give the orders to the others, and Fargo slid down to re[st] against one of the beams holding the stable overhang.

Joseph dropped to one knee beside him. "What else?" Joseph asked, eyeing the big man shrewdly.

"What's that mean?" Fargo returned.

"You thinking of something more, Fargo," Joseph sai[d] "You know that even if we lose no more men, Tarawa wi[ll] win. He has plenty more warriors, plenty time, plenty way[s] to attack."

"That's why I've got to figure a way to turn it aroun[d] somehow," Fargo said.

Further talk was cut off as the sentry shouted down fro[m] the wall. "Here they come again," he called.

"Remember, everybody stay down," Fargo heard th[e] captain shout, and he lifted his gaze to the wall where th[e] defenders crouched down below the top. He saw the fir[st] cluster of arrows fly over them, then two more clusters f[ill] the air. Most of the arrows fell harmlessly to the ground, b[ut] enough embedded themselves into the stockade walls.

Fargo listened, eyes half-closed, and finally heard th[e] Kiowa break off the forays and race away. "Stay dow[n] They'll be back to give it another try," he shouted up to th[e] others as he leaned back against the beam again.

The sound of pounding hoofbeats soon confirmed h[is] warning, and the clustered volleys of arrows filled the a[ir] again until the Kiowa broke off the attack. Captain Roge[rs]

ose to his feet and peered over the wall, and the others fol-
owed his example. He turned away finally and climbed
own to where Fargo had pulled himself up with Joseph
eside him. Major Armsted strode up with a military snap
hat the nervousness in his face denied.

"He'll be mounting a full attack next, I presume," the
major said.

"Not till morning," Fargo said. "He'll rest his braves first,
hen let them work themselves up with chants and war
ances." He felt Captain Rogers' eyes on him and flicked a
lance at the man.

"What do we do?" the captain said.

The major cut in at once. "We defend the fort," he said
ompously. "With everything we have."

"Everything we have won't hold out long," Captain
ogers said. "What do we do, Fargo? I've been watching
ou thinking out something."

"I'm giving the orders here, Captain. This is very close to
 subordination," the major protested.

"We're very close to dead," the captain returned. "What
o we do, Fargo?"

"Give him some of his own medicine, turn his game back
n him," Fargo said.

"Tell us what you want," the captain said.

"All the Conestogas here, every trooper's cap and spare
fle, hammer, nails, and rope," Fargo said.

"You heard the man," the captain barked at the others lis-
ning. "Get to it."

Fargo stepped back and watched Major Armsted stride to
is office, his face wreathed in petulance. The captain
irected the soldiers following Fargo's orders, and the
onestogas were wheeled to the center of the compound.
nder Fargo's direction, the men worked with silent, pur-
oseful speed, and when they finished, the sun had slipped
er the horizon. But Fargo moved back, his eyes narrowed

as he scanned the wagons, much as the Kiowa chief ha
done only a few days before. His eyes saw the line of blu
caps and an occasional ten-gallon hat, the rifle barrel
protruding from above the wagon frame. There was no sig
that the rifles were tied in place and the hats nailed down

"Good," Fargo grunted. "Tarawa will be sure we're try
ing to make a run for it. He'll come barreling down pourin
arrows into the wagons. Now for the other half of his sur
prise." Fargo halted to peer up at the night that drifted ove
the fort. "Tarawa will be working his braves into a frenzy
but he'll have at least one keeping watch. There'll b
enough moon so they'd be sure to see us if we really tried t
sneak out in the night. But from where they are, they ca
only see the front and one side of the fort. Rig up a hal
dozen ropes down the outside of the back wall, stron
enough to hold a man sliding down."

Captain Rogers nodded. "We're going to be outside th
back wall, come dawn," he said.

"Exactly. The wagons will race around the fort and th
Kiowa will go after them. Your men will fire from flat on th
ground. You'll catch them completely by surprise. I'd gues
you'll take out more than half in the first volley," Fargo said

"And when the others turn to fire back, we'll be smal
prone targets damn near impossible to hit. Our second vo
ley ought to get most of the rest," the captain said wit
enthusiasm. He halted, his face tightening. "What if h
smells a rat and doesn't go after the wagons?" he asked.

Fargo half-shrugged. "We're in a lot of trouble," h
answered. "Now let's get those ropes in place." He wer
with the captain as the officer chose six men to tie and lowe
the ropes from the top of the rear wall.

When the task was completed, Fargo had the men turn i
and he lay down on the hay again, slept until the night gre
deep. When he woke, dawn was no more than an hou
away, and he saw Captain Rogers had turned the men ou

wagons waiting behind the closed gates. "Start lowering
men over the wall," Fargo said.

The captain nodded, began to move toward the rear of
stockade when a figure stepped briskly from the bar-
ks building. The major halted before the big man with
lake-blue eyes and tried to look authoritative.

"I am the commander of Fort Calder. If my men are
ng to follow your plan and engage the enemy, I'll lead
m," he said.

"Pick yourself a rope," Fargo said.

The man frowned, almost as if he were disappointed he
dn't received more opposition. He turned and climbed
to the top of the rear wall. The captain followed and the
opers moved after him.

Fargo stayed below and watched as, one by one, the men
vered themselves down the ropes under the captain's
tchful gaze. When the last man had gone over, Captain
gers turned, waved, and swung himself over the top of
wall. Fargo's eyes locked with those of the four settlers
t had elected to drive the wagons. "I'll lead the way," he
d them. "When I stop, take cover under your wagons and
k your targets."

The men nodded and climbed up onto the wagons as
eph appeared leading his own horse and the Ovaro. "I
lead with you," Joseph said.

"No, you stay here out of sight," Fargo said, drawing an
tant frown from the round face. "If it goes wrong, you run
it. Get back to Millicent. Maybe you can help her.
ybe something will go right." Joseph nodded reluctant
eement.

The night suddenly became gray. Fargo waited till the
t pink flush crept across the sky before he swung onto the
aro. He walked the horse to the gates as Joseph slid the
avy bolt. Then Fargo turned, glanced back to those
sed on the driver's seat of each wagon. He raised one

arm high into the air. "Roll 'em hard," he shouted as he se
the Ovaro into a gallop. He raced through the opened gate
glanced back to see the wagons coming after him, the dri
ers snapping their whips over the horses. He turned h
gaze across the prairie: the Kiowa were already on the
ponies and their war whoops carried across the flat land
they began to move forward. Fargo saw the tall, bronze
muscled figure of Tarawa, Thunder Chief, with ar
upraised, a lance in his grip.

Fargo held his course for a few moments longer, the
wheeled the Ovaro in a long circle, the wagons following.
tight smile touched his lips as he saw the Kiowa shift
come after him, certain that he had seen the wago
couldn't go north and had turned them in an effort to esca
their pursuers. Fargo raced the wagons at an angle, usi
up time as the Kiowa closed ground with breakneck spee
He glanced at their racing ponies, counted off seconds, a
sent the wagons careening past the fort. All four wagons h
cleared the rear corner of the fort when the Kiowa sent th
first volley of arrows flying. Completely intent on chasi
the fleeing wagons, the Indians swept past the rear of t
fort without a sideways glance and started to move up
both sides of the wagons when the rifle fire exploded. Far
found himself thinking how sweet a sound rifle fire could
as he reined the Ovaro to a halt and heard the wagons p
up behind him.

He wheeled, saw that his guess had been right. The fi
volley of rifle fire had hit hard and accurately. Taraw
force had been cut down by at least half, and he saw the o
ers wheeling in surprise and confusion. He leapt from t
Ovaro to join a gray-haired man beneath the first wago
the big Sharps in his hand. A buck with one short a
crossed in front of his sights, and he fired. The Kio
seemed to whirl atop his pony before toppling to t
ground. Fargo saw Tarawa racing in circles, shouting a

ganizing his warriors, and the Kiowa gathered to race at
the troopers on the ground. They stayed bunched together
closely and the low-level fire proved devastating; the
Kiowa dropped from their ponies like so many autumn
leaves from a tree. They broke off the attack, scattered, and
Fargo noticed one streaking toward the wagons. He pushed
himself out from beneath the Conestoga, vaulted onto the
Ovaro, and raced out to meet the Indian's charge. The
Kiowa, his shoulder bleeding from a wound, swerved his
way to try to escape, but Fargo crossed his line of flight at a
forty-five-degree angle. He fired on the gallop, the kick of
the big Sharps knocking him backward in the saddle, but he
saw the Kiowa throw up his hands and bring his pony to a
halt.

Fargo rode to the Indian as he threw a glance across the
land. Tarawa and half a dozen of his braves were
streaking toward the horizon, but he saw the Kiowa chief
turn and look back at him. Fargo drew to a halt alongside
the Kiowa, and the Indian dropped his hands as he slowly
turned his pony to face the big man on the Ovaro. His
shoulders seemed to droop in defeat and exhaustion, but
then Fargo caught the quick motion of his right wrist. The
Indian flung a knife in a quick, underhand motion that was
too accurate. Fargo threw himself backward off his horse
the knife hurtled a fraction of an inch past his face. He hit
the ground on his back and shoulders, grunted with the
pain, and whirled to his feet as the Kiowa charged around
the Ovaro. Fargo drew the Colt as the Indian raced at him,
tomahawk raised to throw. He fired and the Kiowa's forehead burst open, exploding in a shower of bone and blood.
The pony raced past, the Kiowa still on its back, spraying
into the air like a moving fountain. He finally fell to the
ground as Fargo stood up.

The Trailsman walked to where the soldiers were
gaining their feet beside the rear wall of the fort.

Captain Rogers came to meet him. "You did it. G[o]
dammit, you did it," the man rejoiced.

"Lose any more men?" Fargo asked.

"Five with minor wounds, one killed," the captain sa[id]
and Fargo caught something in his voice. "Armsted," [the]
captain finished.

"Chickens keep coming home to roost," Fargo grunte[d.]

"I saw him get up and start to run when the Kiowa ma[de]
that last head-on charge at us. Damn fool made himself [the]
only big target. They put eight arrows into him," the ca[p]-
tain said.

Fargo's eyes went past the officer. "The fort's still ther[e,]"
he remarked.

The captain made a wry sound. "It'll still be Armste[d's]
monument," he said bitterly. "You saved it, but he'll get [the]
credit."

"He won't be enjoying it," Fargo said.

Joseph rode up, a silent message in his black eyes, a[s]
Fargo pulled himself onto the Ovaro.

"Where are you going? A lot of people want to tha[nk]
you." Captain Rogers frowned.

"You do the honors for me. Got another kind of party [to]
go to," Fargo said. He waved as he sent the horse into a [fast]
trot across the flat land. Joseph came up to ride beside h[im]
in a moment. "One down, one to go," Fargo commente[d.]

"Got bad feeling," Joseph grunted.

"You're a damn pessimist," Fargo growled, and reme[m]-
bered how right Joseph had been about big trouble all co[m]-
ing at once. He swore under his breath as he spurred [the]
horse into a faster pace.

go and Joseph had ridden through the night with but a
short stops to rest the horses, and it was just past dawn
en they reached Spineyleaf, the town still mostly asleep.
go drew up before the small white house and slid from
saddle. His lips tightened as he saw the front door splin-
ed, the lock blown away by a bullet. He had the big Colt
and as he pushed the door open with his foot. Stepping
de simply confirmed what he knew he'd find. The
rsely furnished living room showed signs of a brief strug-
one of the high-backed chairs smashed into bits, two
es lying in pieces on the floor, the lamp on its side in
corner.

Damn her hide," Fargo swore angrily.

Maybe they just came and took her," Joseph said.

argo shot him a pained glance. "You know better.
y'd no reason. She couldn't wait. She went out trying to
to Mai-lin on her own. They caught her and came back
e for the old man."

oseph's nod was unhappy agreement. "We go after her?"
asked.

Not till dark," Fargo said. "Let's find a couple of beds

and get some real rest till then." He strode through the
ing room, found a bed in a guest room for Joseph
another for himself. He stretched out and exhaus
brought sleep almost at once. But not before he brought
Colt from its holster and curled it under his hand beside
pillow.

The warm sun that slipped into the room didn't w
him, and he slept soundly till night fell. Joseph was in
living room when he finished washing and came out, a ti
chipped beef on the table. "Found it in kitchen," Jos
said as he took another forkful.

Fargo took a bite and leaned back in the chair and sp
his thoughts. "The old mine, they'd take her there."

"Maybe gone already," Joseph said.

Fargo shook away the possibility, unwilling to accep
"They've only had her a day or two," he said. "She didn
nosing around till after you saw her." He rose, tightened
gun belt, and finished what Joseph left of the chipped b
"We'll make a stop along the way," he said.

"Thorenson's place?" Joseph said.

Fargo nodded. Joseph followed him outside to the ho
and Fargo led the way through town and east toward
Wasatch foothills. They rode steadily east until they nea
the foothills; then they turned up onto the high land wh
they could stay out of sight and yet see the slave trad
house.

Moonlight laid a pale glow across the land as Thorens
ranch house came into sight just below, but lamps tur
high formed a yellow square of light around the en
house. Two coaches were lined up outside in front of
house; one a country brougham with twin lamps, d
doors, and curtained windows; the other a Clarence r
away sitting high over its oversized, thin wheels,
roofline projecting over the driver's seat with shades l

led down on its wide windows. Both were fancy coaches
this part of the territory.

oseph questioned with his eyes and Fargo grunted the
ly. "I'd say Thorenson's buyers have arrived," he said.
's entertaining. Maybe they've seen the girls already,
maybe not. Either way I'm changing their plans."

You want me to watch the house?" Joseph said.

I want you to get some extra horses. I've a feeling we're
ng to need them, at least two. Think you can do it,
eph?" Fargo asked.

Can beaver swim?" Joseph muttered.

After you get the horses, go to the mine. Hang back.
y out of sight," Fargo said.

You going in?"

Right. When I get out, I'll want you and the horses
ting."

What if you don't come out, Fargo?" Joseph inquired
tter-of-factly.

Give me till morning. I don't come out, you do whatev-
best. Don't put your neck in a noose."

Same to you," Joseph replied as he dismounted and
ted downhill, leading his sturdy horse behind. When he
appeared into the dark and the trees, Fargo moved on
ng the high ground until he reached the old mine. He
ped from the saddle and dropped to a crouch as he
ved closer to the entrance. Tethering the Ovaro in the
es, he crept forward and spotted the single figure
rding the mouth of the shaft. He let his gaze slowly trav-
e the sides of the mine, but there were no other sentries
ted and he returned his gaze to the man by the entrance.
orenson felt secure. The lamps inside the shaftway
re lighted, the soft glow outlining the man's figure.
go moved closer, waited till the sentry turned his
d away, and darted forward to press himself against the
k side of the old mine. He waited a moment and then

started toward the entrance of the mine, his back pres
against the rocks until he halted and swore silently. F
crept as close as he could unseen. A side or rock protru
outward, and to reach the sentry he'd have to move aro
it into the open. Only a few feet, yet more than enough t
for the man to draw his gun and fire.

Fargo's lips pulled back in a grimace. Noise was the
thing he couldn't allow. Trying to slide around
protruding piece of rock would only give the guard n
time to see him and react. He'd have to leap into view
strike almost in one motion. He drew the Colt from its
ster, grasped the gun by the barrel. Tensing every mu
of his powerful thighs, he sprang forward into the op
whirled as he did. The sentry blinked in surprise, froze f
split second before reaching for his gun. But the split
ond was delay enough. Fargo dived and smashed the bu
the Colt into the man's forehead. He heard the soun
bone shattering, and the sentry crumpled to the groun

Fargo dragged him into the old mine as he pushed
crossed boards aside. He saw the lamps burning all the
down the shaft and pulled the inert form behind him a
went down the shored tunnel. When he reached the
ondary shaftway he'd noticed when he first explored the
mine, he dragged the guard into it and threw his still f
into the blackness of the unlighted tunnel. He hurried l
to the main shaft and moved down its narrow passage, si
as a cougar on the prowl. He slowed as he reached
rusted mine cart that marked the large, circular area car
out inside the mine. He halted, dropped to one knee as
area came into sight. The manacles against the walls
longer hung empty. Two girls—one Asian, the other bro
skinned—hung shackled to the manacles: their hair stri
torn, cheap dresses covering young, lithe bodies; their f
dulled by defeat and despair.

He scanned the other wall of the circular area to

illie, tied to a chair and gagged. Near her, on another hair, Mr. Soong sat with wrists bound, his parchment face xpressionless. Fargo eyes swung to the wire cage. A girl sat side it on a small stool. He needed no introduction to now who she was; a pale-blue Oriental dress of one piece ith a slit up the side clung to a beautifully curved figure, it her face held his gaze, black hair hanging almost to her aist, high yet soft cheekbones, no angles to her, beauti-lly shaped lips below a tiny, delicate nose, a sloe-eyed veliness that was almost breathtaking. He watched Mai-1 as she moved on the stool, put her hands in her lap. She ight well have been sitting in relaxed meditation were it ot for the cage around her. Delicacy and strength, he ecided as his eyes stayed on her. She looked up, her eyes oving around the area, deep-black pupils that shimmered ith deep fires.

He took his eyes from her with an effort, scanning the ooden table in the middle of the circular area. A heavy ng holding a half-dozen keys was in the center of the table. argo moved forward in quick, half-crouched steps and saw lillicent's eyes grow wide as he came forward. He scooped e key ring from the table and saw a flicker of emotion cross Ir. Soong's face. He paused at Millicent and pulled the gag om her mouth. He started to untie the ropes at her ankles hen the voice drifted across the circular area.

"Don't touch her, mister," it said, soft and deadly. Fargo oze in motion. "Don't try for your gun. You're covered."

Fargo slowly straightened and turned. The man in the irty brown vest held a big Walker Colt. Fargo suddenly emed small next to the mountainous figure beside him, a uge man, bare-chested, a pair of loose pants that reached nly halfway down his thighs his only clothing. Fargo met e glittering dark eyes that stared at him from a flat-nosed, road Mongol face with a shaven head.

"Kwang," he heard Millicent say.

133

"Figured that out myself," Fargo said without taking [his] eyes from the mountain with legs. The Mongol was at le[ast] six feet, six inches, he estimated, plenty of flesh on him b[ut] with a massive muscular structure under it: arms that we[re] small trees, legs that could have come from a Percheron.

"We expected you might show," the man in the vest sa[id.] "That's why we left one sentry outside. We figured you[r] get suspicious if nobody was on guard." He grinned a[nd] Fargo cursed silently at the accuracy of his words. "Dr[op] the gun belt," Thorenson's man said. Fargo obeye[d,] deciding the Walker was too close to miss. "Back off," t[he] man growled, and Fargo moved back almost behi[nd] Millicent's chair. The man reached down, yanked the C[olt] from the gun belt, and retreated. He motioned with his ow[n] gun. "Sit down, the other side of the cage," he ordered, a[nd] Fargo walked past the cage and met Mai-lin's eyes. The[y] showed interest and admiration, he saw, calm pride and [no] fear at all.

He lowered himself to the hard ground on the other si[de] of the cage. Thorenson's man stepped to the two shackl[ed] girls, lifted each one's head up, and gave each a grin. Far[go] drew his knees up high and wrapped his arms around t[he] bottom of his legs just above the ankle. He shifted his po[si-] tion to turn his right leg away from Kwang. Thorenso[n's] man was checking the shackles on the two girls as Farg[o's] hand stole up the inside of his trousers, reached the smoo[th] leather of the calf holster stropped to his leg. He pushed t[he] double-edged throwing blade out of the holster and let [it] drop into his hand as Thorenson's man turned aroun[d.] Fargo pressed the blade against his leg out of the man's li[ne] of sight.

"I'd kill you now, but I know Thorenson will want to ta[lk] to you first," the man said. "So we'll just put some iron cu[ffs] on you. Get up."

Fargo slowly started to obey, half-turned his leg, an[d]

ery muscle of shoulder and arm tightened, flung the
.de with one lightning-fast, underhand motion. The thin,
.uble-edged throwing knife hurtled through the air with
.mendous force. The man saw it, tried to twist aside, but
was too late. The razor-sharp blade plunged into his solar
.xus, just below his ribs. It disappeared to the hilt, and
.rgo was on his feet, running forward as the man bent
.er, his eyes bulging, his mouth dropping open. He
.sped both hands to the hilt of the knife, gasped as he
.ed to pull it free. But strength had already left him and he
.de small croaking noises as he fell forward to his knees,
.ayed there for a moment, and then pitched onto his stom-
.a, driving the blade in deeper.

.Fargo had almost reached the gun that fell from the man's
.nd when he saw Kwang's leg move, the big foot kick the
.n away and send it spinning across the ground to the far
.ll. Fargo halted, his eyes lifting upward to see the huge
.ongol in front of him. The man's flat, broad face broke into
.low grin of sadistic anticipation; he flexed the muscles of
. treelike arms, opened and closed his huge hands.
.wang kill you," the mountain rasped and lurched toward
.n.

.Fargo backed away in a half-circle and suddenly stopped,
.ing on the balls of his feet as he shot out a wicked left and
.lowed with a right thrown up with every ounce of
.ength in his powerful shoulders. Both blows landed flush
. the Mongol's jaw, and Fargo saw him stop and blink, but
.n the grin on his face grew wider as he moved forward
.ain.

.Fargo let the huge man come closer, feinted, threw a
.rd right. Kwang's arm came up with surprising quickness
. fend off the blow, followed with a downward, hammer-
.e blow that Fargo easily ducked under. Kwang stepped
.ward, threw another punch, a looping blow that Fargo
.ain ducked. A roar flew from the mountain of flesh as

Kwang sprang forward, his bulk moving with surprisi[ng] quickness.

Fargo set himself and brought up a tremendous upper[cut] that caught the huge man at the point of the jaw. It wa[s a] blow that would have felled most men instantly. Kwa[ng] staggered back a few steps and swung an arm in a backwa[rd] blow. Fargo lifted his arm, parried the blow, and was flu[ng] sideways by the force of it. He whirled as Kwang rushed [at] him, the great arms outstretched. Once again Far[go] stepped inside the huge arms to deliver a tremendous ri[ght] hook. Kwang's head half-turned from the force of the blo[w] but his forward momentum didn't even falter. Fargo hu[r]tled backward as the huge Mongol slammed into him. [He] twisted away from one blow but another smashed do[wn] across the back of his neck.

The sheer force of it knocked him to his hands and kne[es] and he shook his head to clear away exploding lights. A hu[ge] arm locked itself around his neck and he was lifted as thou[gh] he were a child, swung in an arc, and sent crashing into t[he] stone wall. He managed to get his forearms up to keep [his] face from slamming against the stones and sank to one kn[ee] as the huge arm pulled away. Fargo started to turn wh[en] the next blow smashed into the small of his back; he gasp[ed] out in pain as he went down again, rolling onto his side t[his] time. He glimpsed the broad face bend down as Kwa[ng] went to grasp hold of his leg, and Fargo drew back, kick[ed] with all his power. The broad face staggered backwar[d], blood suddenly streaming from the flat cheekbones a[nd] from the mouth that no longer grinned sadistically.

The massive Mongol let out a roar of rage as he leapt f[or]ward, both arms outstretched. Fargo rolled and almost g[ot] free of the leaping mountain, but one arm came down o[n] the side of his head and a blanket of gray immediate[ly] dropped over his eyes. He rolled again, shook his head cle[ar] in time to see the huge fist driving at him. He dropped, b[ut] e blow caught him glancingly across the forehead. It was ough to send him sprawling, and once more the huge an was atop him. Fargo was lifted and held by one huge and while Kwang brought a blow up from below and ammed it into his body. Fargo flew back doubled over, ruck the wall, and fell to the ground. He felt as if he'd een broken in two, the pain a searing explosion inside him. ut the pain fueled desperate fury, generating raw reserves strength deep inside him. Kwang came forward, huge ms raised, waiting for his opponent to try to rise again. argo gathered the power of his thighs, kept his head down, d half-dived, half-leapt, closing his arms around one tre- endous leg and yanking with all the power he had within im. Pulled off balance, the mountainous form crashed to e ground as the old mine shook with the impact.

Fargo let go of the leg, leapt forward, and brought a blow p to crash against Kwang's face as the man rolled to regain s feet. The blow split the skin of the already bloodied face d opened a new stream of red; Fargo followed with a loop- g left that connected. Kwang fell to one knee and rose at ce, another roar erupting from the massive chest. Fargo lt the weariness in his arms as he connected with a straight ft and a right. Kwang blinked and came forward. Fargo hit im with another tremendous right and felt the pain of it in s own shoulder muscles. The Mongol shook off the blow, ared again. Fargo tried to twist away from the long arms at reached for him. He spun, slipped, and felt a forearm circle his neck. He pulled himself down, almost onto his ees, and slipped out of the grip, but the blow that came om behind him sent him flying almost into the wall.

Fargo saw the edge of the old, overturned mine cart eside him as he tried to get to his feet. Kwang's massive rm charged toward him, and Fargo tried to back and circle gain. But his body cried out in pain, his shoulders and arms most numb with weariness. He lifted his arms to parry

another tremendous blow and was slammed back dow
from the force of it. Kwang was on him at once, the blood
smeared face a hideous apparition. Fargo got another dri
ing blow in, this time digging into the man's stomach, but
seemed to have no effect. He felt himself lifted and flun
into the side of the overturned old mine cart. He bounce
from the cart, fell to the ground, and his outstretched han
touched something—the wooden handle of a rusted pick
with only one prong still attached.

Kwang's massive shape loomed over him, the treelik
arms reached out. Fargo closed his hand over the handle
the broken pickax. With every last ounce of strength h
brought the stout wooden handle around in an arc to slam
into the Mongol's hip. Kwang let out a roar of pain as h
staggered back, fell to one knee, one hand going to his hi
where a stream of red cascaded. Fargo pushed himself to h
feet and saw Kwang start to get up, fall back on one knee a
the shattered hipbone gave way. Raging in fury, the Mong
rose again and came at him, dragging one leg behind hin
insensate rage overcoming all else.

Fargo swung the weapon again as Kwang reached him
He used the one-half of the pickax still on the handle an
drove the rusted point into the massive chest. Kwan
roared with the rage of a mortally wounded bull, staggere
back as his massive chest grew red at once. But he remaine
on his feet.

"Goddammit," Fargo swore aloud as he swung the
again. He held it with both hands this time, brought th
weapon around in a flat arc. The huge Mongol's shattere
hip gave way again and he dropped to one knee just
Fargo's blow reached him. The pickax slammed into h
head, all but severing it from his neck with an explosion
blood, tissue, and bone that flew high enough to spatter th
shored-up ceiling.

Fargo heard Millicent's choked-off scream, but his eye

ayed on the mountainous form collapsed on the ground.
his time it stayed motionless, not unlike a slaughtered bull
at turned the ground red around it.

Fargo let the ax drop from his hands as he leaned back
ainst the wall and gasped in deep breaths. He slid to the
ound to rest and felt his wind returning. He rose finally
d met the stares of the girls, still hanging from the
anacles.

Millicent's voice called to him. "That pail in the corner,
ere's water in it."

He moved across the clearing, his body wincing with
ch step. He sank to his knees beside the pail, dipped his
ad into the cold water, and held it there as long as his
eath allowed. He gave himself another minute and then
shed himself to his feet. His body protested, but he felt
s muscles obeying again. He retrieved his throwing knife
om Thorenson's man, wiped it clean on the brown vest,
d picked his Colt up from against the wall. He untied
illicent and motioned to the keys on the table. "Open
ose manacles," he told her as he pulled the door of the
ge open.

Mai-lin stepped out. She seemed smaller, more delicate
an she had inside the cage. And even more beautiful in
at very special way that was her own stamp. Her sloe eyes
ld his and she spoke, her voice velvet, as sensual as the
rk-fire eyes. "You are Fargo," she said. "Millicent told
e you might come. You are *hao jan chih ch'i*."

"Something tells me I should say thanks," Fargo said.
ut right now we'd best get the hell out of here." He
arted to turn when he heard voices from the other end of
e shaft. "In that corner," he said, motioning to everyone
he drew the Colt. He watched Mai-lin follow her father
to the far corner before he turned away and took up a posi-
n just behind the edge of the shaft where it opened onto
e circular area. The voices grew louder—three men, he

139

counted, one of them Thorenson. He waited as the figure
stepped around the end of the shaft, Thorenson first, th
man halting, his frown instant.

Fargo stepped forward, the Colt leveled at him. "Su
prise," he growled.

Thorenson's eyes turned to him, naked hatred in h
stare. The other two men, both well dressed, both portl
showed only fright in their clean-shaven faces. "You mu
be crazy. You won't get away with this," Thorenson said.

"I've heard that before. Drop your gun," Fargo said, an
Thorenson lifted his gun from its holster and let it fall to th
ground. "Manacle them," Fargo said to Millicent. Sh
spoke to one of the other two girls and the girl hurried wit
her as Fargo motioned the men against the wall. The gi
snapped the manacle on Thorenson and then stepped bac
Before anyone could stop her, she kicked him in the gro
and he screamed in pain as he sank to his knees, only th
manacles keeping him up. "Jesus, oh, Jesus," Thorenso
gasped as he hung from his manacled wrists. Millice
pulled the girl back and manacled the other two men l
herself.

One of the two men, a gray waistcoat under his jacke
summoned enough courage to find his voice. "Thorenson
men will be coming along. They'll turn us loose," he sai
"They'll go after you then."

"I'm real upset about that," Fargo said.

Thorenson lifted his head and Fargo again saw hatre
through the pain in his eyes. The soft, thick, fleshy lips th
didn't belong in the blocklike face opened enough f
Thorenson to hiss the words. "Dead . . . you're dead. M
men coming . . . I'll get you for this," he breathed. "De
. . . you're dead."

Fargo turned from the man in disgust. But the sla
trader was right about one thing, he realized: his me
would be arriving. Fargo motioned to Millicent and the ot

ers. He didn't want to be trapped in a shoot-out that could end the wrong way. He started up the old mine shaft as the others followed: Millicent and Mai-lin flanking Mr. Soong, the two girls close behind. He halted when he reached the entrance of the shaft to peer into the night. The dark was silent and he moved outside, the Colt in his hand, waving the others on. He dropped to one knee as he caught movement at the edge of the trees, the big Colt .45 ready to fire. Joseph came into sight and Fargo sighed in relief. Joseph led three horses behind his brown mare, one the gray gelding. He tossed the reins to Millicent as she hurried to the horse.

"Nice work, Joseph," Fargo said. He turned to the old man. "Can you ride?" he asked.

Mr. Soong nodded. "Slowly," he said.

"Help him on," Fargo said, and saw Millicent and Mai-lin hurry to obey. He turned back to Joseph. "They'll come after us. We'll split up. You take Soong and the two girls. There's a U.S. marshal in Split Rock. Let Soong and the two girls fill him in."

"You?" Joseph asked.

"It's Mai-lin he wants back most. I'm going to hide out in the barracks Schoonmaker used at the base of the Wind River Range," Fargo said. "Give the marshal a chance to take in Thorenson."

Joseph nodded and Fargo saw Millicent speak to the Asian girl, who nodded understanding and climbed aboard the other horse. The brown-skinned girl climbed up behind her. Fargo pulled himself onto the Ovaro as Millicent took the gray. "Mai-lin will ride with me," she said with pointed firmness.

Fargo shrugged. "We'll start together, split up a mile or so on," he said to Joseph. He took the lead, only a few paces ahead of the others, and steered a course up the side of the low hills that would be easy to spot by anyone following. He halted when they reached a dense stand of balsam where the ground lay thick with soft needles. "Good luck, Joseph," he said, and received a nod in return. He waited to watch Joseph move off through the balsams with the others following.

"He'll have to go slow. They'll surely catch up to him," Millicent said. "Maybe we should all stick together."

"Then there's no doubt they'll catch up to us," Fargo said. "Joseph will cover his tracks. They'll go in circles trying to find him. Meanwhile, we make time." He sent the Ovaro into a fast canter, north away from the direction Joseph had taken. After a few hours he turned and headed down to the river. He reached it as dawn streaked the sky, halted to let the horses rest and drink. He was tearing off a low branch thick with leaves when Millicent paused beside him as she refilled her canteen. "What did she say to me back in the mine?" he asked, nodding to where Mai-lin waited by the gray.

"*Hao jan chih ch'i?*" Millicent said. "That means you are a man of special greatness."

"Good judge of character, that girl," Fargo said, and heard Millicent's disdainful little sniff. "You don't agree with her?" He grinned.

"First, Mai-lin's very young, very impressionable," Millicent said.

"And very beautiful," Fargo remarked.

Millicent tossed a sharp glance at him. "The phrase has a special meaning in Chinese philosophy. If she knew the other side of you, she wouldn't have used it."

"Hell, she might mean it even more if she did." He laughed, and ignored Millicent's glare as he swung onto the Ovaro, the leafy branch in his hand. "Get your horse into the river," he said, and waited as Millicent mounted and Mai-lin swung up behind her. The slitted, one-piece Oriental dress rode up as Mai-lin took to the saddle, and he noted

142

the beautifully formed, graceful line of her legs. Millicent took the gray gelding into the river and he followed on the Ovaro. He leaned sideways in the saddle to sweep the riverbank with the leafy branch, obliterating the hoofprints. When he finished, he crossed the other side and swept the far bank with the branch.

"We didn't leave any prints there," Millicent said.

It was Mai-lin's voice that answered. "They see same signs of wiping away marks on that side and think we crossed over," she said. "Very clever."

Fargo turned a wide smile to her. "You've got it. That's exactly what they'll think and they'll lose a half-day looking for us, more backtracking," Fargo said. "How'd you like to become a trailsman, honey?"

Mai-lin's little laugh was a low giggle full of sensuous warmth. Her smile was made of admiration, Millicent's glance made of cool approval. He headed the Ovaro into midriver and turned the horse upstream. "We'll let the horses swim some and walk some on the shallow ground near the bank. But make sure you stay in the water," he said.

"I quite understand. I'm not a child," Millicent snapped.

"I don't know what you are, honey," Fargo growled. "Joseph had to pull my message out of you."

"You went off. You knew how I felt about that," she returned.

"So you had to be a real little bitch," he threw back.

"Bitch? What is that?" Mai-lin asked.

"Tell her," Fargo dared.

Millicent spoke over her shoulder to Mai-lin. "Fargo was to stay here and help save you. Instead, he went off to do something else," she said stiffly.

"Try telling it right," Fargo growled, his eyes turning to Mai-lin. "A hundred people were going to be killed. I went to try to save them."

"At your expense," Millicent snapped to the girl.

"Fargo did what he thought best," Mai-lin said soberly, her dark eyes staying on the big man.

"You don't understand," Millicent said.

"I'd say she understands damn well." Fargo grinned.

Millicent simmered in silence and Fargo moved the Ovaro past her to the shallow water and let him find firm ground. Millicent pulled the gray gelding alongside and Fargo kept the horses moving at a steady pace. The sun burned down but the cool of the water took the enervating power out of it and Fargo kept the horses moving forward. The sun had slipped into the afternoon sky when Millicent called out.

"Can't we stop? We haven't slept in twenty-four hours," she said.

"You'll have plenty time to sleep when we reach the cabins," Fargo growled. "Keep moving."

Millicent's full lips tightened, but she didn't argue further. Fargo led the way around a curve in the river. He'd gone on for another hour when he saw the river grow narrow, the sharp turn just ahead. "Keep going and don't look sideways," he ordered.

Millicent's lips tightened and he saw she was glad to obey, kept her eyes staring straight ahead as they rounded the narrow curve and he took her past the remains of Bill Schoonmaker's platoon. He slowed when they had gone far enough to lose the odor that still lingered by the bend. The low hills of the Wind River Range had just come into sight when he felt the Ovaro's legs noticeably tiring. He pulled the horse out of the river on the bank where a wedge of good bluestem grew in thick profusion. Millicent followed and the horses attacked the grass with hungry eagerness as soon as everyone dismounted.

Fargo watched Millicent sink wearily to the ground as Mai-lin knelt at the riverbank and dipped her hands into the

er, wet her face and neck with the cool liquid. She rose
folded herself onto the grass near Millicent, every
ement graceful, her slender body fluid; her smallish,
breasts were completely right on her.

argo moved into the dark shadows under the trees and
ed back against a willow, his glance moving over the
young women. Millicent's almost blond hair glinted soft
ks under the sun, her full breasts jutted hard against
white shirt, her thin nose and full, red lips turned to the
she was the embodiment of strong, cool loveliness.
-lin's supple, lithe, slender body seemed to curve,
ugh she sat up straight, jet-black hair hanging full down
back, her smooth, fine-featured face wreathed in a calm
se. Different kinds of beauty, Fargo observed—
icent soft yellows, Mai-lin dark violet, marigold and
ng gentian. Different inside as well as outside—
icent working hard to hold on to her unbending stiff-
, her eyes flicking to him with contained coolness;
-lin glancing with soft warmth and open admiration.

he horses still grazed hungrily and Fargo moved back
per under the trees and stretched out on a mat of dark-
n nut moss. He closed his eyes, but he sat up at once as
t sound drifted from across the river. He saw the three
emen move onto the far bank. His eyes narrowed as he
in the three men—drifters, range rats, he saw at once.
es and clothes marked them: shifty eyes, cur-dog faces,
adbare, worn outfits with cracked-leather gun belts.
se were men used to scrounging and biting their way
ugh life. But, like coyotes, they were quick to see an
ortunity. Fargo pushed himself deeper into the trees,
ng out of sight as the three riders started across the
r.

Well, look at what we've found," the first one said, a
-eyed man with a long tear across the brim of his hat.
illicent was on her feet instantly and whirled to peer

into the trees, fright in her face. "Fargo," she called in a
as the three men emerged onto the bank and dismount

"We've got us a nice filly and a China doll." Torn
grinned.

Mai-lin moved closer to Millicent. "Get away from
We're not alone," Millicent said, glaring at the three n
Torn Hat's hard eyes flicked to the gray and the Ovaro

"Don't see another horse, honey." He grinned.

Millicent whirled to the trees, anger mixing with fea
her face. "Fargo, where are you, dammit?" she cal
waited, turned back to the men. "He's here, I tell you,"
said.

. "Sure, you've got the whole cavalry here. Good
doll," the man said, laughing.

Fargo swore inwardly as he moved in silence. Tl
could be no shooting. More than one reason: this was
Kiowa territory, and he'd no way of knowing if Thorens
men were near enough to hear. A shot would echo pl
far down the river. He had to take the three scroun
before they could draw and shoot, and there would be
one way to do that. He'd let human nature, the worst sic
it, be his ally.

He swept the woods as he moved on silent steps thro
the trees and came to a halt when he spotted the lengt
half-rotted log. He pulled away the crumpled end and it
a jagged protrusion of wood that hadn't rotted away yet.
have to do, he muttered inwardly as he lifted the piec
log and moved forward to drop to one knee at the edg
the trees. He waited and watched the scene exploc
before his eyes. Millicent tried to whirl and run for the g
ing, but Torn Hat brought her down with a tackle. On
the other two seized Mai-lin and held her from behind

"Let me go," Millicent screamed, and tried to rake
nails across the man's face. He avoided the blow, yar
hard, and she slid forward, her skirt riding up.

146

ook at those pins," Torn Hat said as he fought off
cent's blows. "Gimme a hand with this little hellcat,"
elled. The third one rushed forward, seized Millicent's
ts, and yanked her arms up over her head. Fargo heard
ry of pain. Torn Hat was grinning as he dropped to his
es and forced Millicent's legs apart. He reached under
skirt as Millicent twisted and screamed, and he had to
o her ankle to pull her back. "Goddamn little bitch," he
e.

ai-lin, Fargo saw, had closed her eyes. The man hold-
er moved closer, his eyes bulging with anticipation.
Iurry up, give it to her. Jesus, I want some of that." He
hed.

argo rose. He'd seen enough, the time was at hand. The
e drifters were thoroughly intent, absorbed in their
sure, lust sweeping away all other senses. He slipped
double-edged throwing knife from its calf-holster and
ped the hilt between his teeth. Digging his heels into
ground, he used its firm softness as a springboard to leap
ard. He was racing at top speed when he broke into the
, long legs driving furiously across the ground. The
e men neither saw, nor heard, nor sensed him as they
hed and drooled and loosened their eager organs.
icent was screaming and sobbing as Torn Hat started to
r himself over her. Fargo, holding the log in front of
in battering-ram fashion, reached the trio. The one
ing Millicent's wrists came into line first and Fargo
med the log into the back of his head. The man pitched
ard soundlessly, half over Millicent. Torn Hat, his trou-
opened, had time only to look up in astonishment as the
struck him full in the face.

e fell backward with a roar of pain through suddenly
d-filled lips. Fargo stumbled, caught hold of the for-
l momentum of his body, and spun around. He let the
all as he dropped the throwing knife from between his

teeth and caught it in one deft motion. The man ho
Mai-lin flung her aside and went for his gun. He had it
half out of its holster when the thin blade whistled int
base of his throat. His mouth fell open to gasp for air
spouted blood. Fargo didn't wait to see him collapse
whirled. Torn Hat had started to pull himself to his fee
face a red smear. Fargo scooped up the log and swu
with all his strength. The man's head swiveled, the cra
his neck a sharp sound as he fell.

Fargo straightened up and felt the pain in his arms
shoulders, the still-lingering effect of his battle with
mountainous Mongol. He saw Millicent on her feet, pu
her disarrayed clothes straight. "Think I cut out on y
He grinned.

"I didn't know what to think," she glared. "Why d
you come when I called you the first time?"

"Didn't want a shoot-out," he said calmly. "I wante
their attention on you."

"So you let me be almost raped," she snapped.

"Almost doesn't count," he said.

"You could've stepped in sooner," she muttered.

"Matter of judgment," he said mildly, and saw Ma
come up to stand before him.

"You are very special, all right," she murmured, her
eyes grave.

"I try." He grinned and turned to Millicent. "Hit the
dle," he said as dusk slid its lavender veil over the hills
swung onto the Ovaro and turned away from the r
Time was most important now, and he headed in
toward the Wind River foothills and let Millicent and
lin follow. He set a fast pace and searched the hills i
fading light to find the twin cabins. He spotted them j
night swept the last of the dusk aside. He swerved up a
slope and heard Millicent follow the sound of his ho
He reached the twin cabins, a dense half-circle of whi

ehind them, and slid to the ground. In the nearest cabin
e found a lamp and had it lighted and turned up as
Iillicent halted the gelding outside. He stepped out and
anded the lamp to her. "Find the lamp in the other cabin.
ou'll find one there, I'm sure. I'll see to the horses," he
aid.

He saw a canvas stretched behind the two cabins to form
crude sun-and-rain shelter, and he unsaddled the horses
id gave them enough tether to let them reach the good
ountain grass nearby. He brought Millicent's saddlebag
ack with him and found she had the lamp lighted in the
her cabin. She stepped outside and handed his lamp back.
ai-lin came to stand beside her.

"We will talk tomorrow, Fargo," she said in her velvet
pice, and her soft, dark orbs sparkled at him. She turned to
llow Millicent into the cabin, the shadow of a smile touch-
g her lips.

He frowned as he went into the next cabin and closed the
por. He shed clothes, turned the lamp out, and stretched
much of his powerful body on the bunk bed as it would
low. Despite the tiredness that engulfed him, he found
mself thinking of Mai-lin and the smile he saw in those
rk orbs. He couldn't help wondering if he were imagining
omises in the depths of those almond-shaped eyes. Some-
ing had simmered there. Something. He went to sleep
ll wondering.

8

The morning sun came in through the single window
wake Fargo. He pulled on trousers and gun belt a
stepped from the cabin. A gray-white mist lay across
slope, slowly coming apart in wisps of haze. The sun bur
with a promise of a hot day to come. His keen ears caugh
sound and he followed it past the adjoining cabin to se
brook bubbling its way down through the white firs.
stepped into the cool of the trees, undressed, and wash
When he finished, the sun had lifted itself higher in the
and broken through the leaves to form ragged patches
warmth. He lay down in one and let the warmth dry
body. He'd rested for perhaps a half-hour and the sun h
long since done its work when he heard the cabin d
opening.

He rose, pulled on trousers and gun belt, and returned
the two cabins to see Mai-lin, her long black hair shining
the sun. The pale-blue, form-fitting gown outlined the s
ple slenderness of her body, the narrow waist that curv
into the long hips, the smallish breasts high, twin lit
mounds of unbroken smoothness under the dress. S
turned as he approached, and he saw her dark eyes m

oss the muscular powerfulness of his shoulders, travel
vn his chest. He stopped before her and she reached out,
:ed the palm of her hand against his pectoral muscles, a
ch both tentative and firm. She ran her hand slowly
vn over his torso and her eyes lifted to meet his.

Beautiful," Mai-lin murmured. "Beautiful." A tiny smile
ched her lips. "Is it wrong to call a man beautiful?" she
ed almost slyly.

We don't do it much here, but I don't guess it's wrong,"
go said.

Her hand moved across his chest again when Millicent's
:e cut through the air with the sharpness of a knifeblade.

Mai-lin! What are you doing?" she called, and hurried
of the cabin doorway, wrapping a dark-blue robe around
self.

Talking to Fargo, Millicent," Mai-lin said softly.

You were touching him," Millicent corrected severely.

The hands can talk," Mai-lin replied quietly, her eyes
ing on the big black-haired man.

That's quite enough hand-talk," Millicent said.

There's a stream back there," Fargo said.

Good," Mai-lin said quickly. "And I see flowers on the
. I must prepare for tonight."

Prepare for what?" Fargo asked.

he dark eyes turned to him. "When I shall come to
," Mai-lin said.

urprise kindled a slow smile that spread across Fargo's
e and he heard Millicent's appalled exclamation. "Mai-
what are you saying?" she flung out.

Mai-lin turned to her. "I must go to Fargo tonight," she
l. "He has saved my life and my father's life."

Oh, no, no, Mai-lin," Millicent said. "You don't have to
anything more for that."

But you know what the book of Chuang Tzü says," the

151

girl answered. "To one who has risked his life for yours must give your most precious gift . . . yourself."

"I know what the book of Chuang Tzü says, but you'r[e] America now. That's not necessary," Millicent answe[red] severely.

"America . . . China . . . time and place are of no im[por]tance. I am bound to give myself. Anything less would [be] dishonor," Mai-lin said.

"No, no, no," Millicent snapped in exasperation. "[You] don't have to do anything of the kind. It's not done he[re.]" She flung a glance at Fargo. "Tell her it's not done he[re,]" she said.

Fargo let his brows lift. "I couldn't exactly say that," answered. "I mean, it is done sometimes."

"Damn you, tell her you don't expect it," Milli[c] snapped.

"I don't expect anything, but I wouldn't want to stop [her] from doing what she feels should be done," he said bland[ly].

Millicent threw a furious glare at him. "Oh, you'd [like] that, wouldn't you?" she accused, and he returned a h[elp]less shrug. She turned to Mai-lin. "We'll talk more ab[out] this," she said severely. "Let's wash and dress now."

She brushed past Fargo with an angry glance as she w[ent] into the cabin and returned carrying towels and hairbrus[hes] in her arms. Mai-lin followed as she stalked away to find [a] little brook.

Fargo sat down on the doorstep and scanned the sl[ope] and the trees that covered most of it. Songbirds and d[oves] moved through the woods as the sun burned away the la[st of] the mist. He listened to the sounds of the two young wo[men] splashing in the brook and heard them finally leave [the] water. He rose and took the big Sharps from his saddle[,] examined the rifle, and cleaned away the road dust that [had] found its way into the long holster. He sighted the [gun] down the slope and swung it in a wide arc before puttin[g]

ack into the holster. Trouble from Thorenson or his men
ould most likely come up the slope, and the cabin let him
over the entire hillside. He could pick them off easily, the
ought reassuring.

He stepped into the doorway as Millicent came around
e corner of the other cabin, her face angry. Mai-lin fol-
owed, her face quietly composed. They went into the cabin
d Fargo heard the door slammed shut.

The sound of voices drifted to him, Millicent's angry, ris-
g and falling and flaring in anger again. Mai-lin's voice
ame as an occasional quiet murmur, the thick cabin doors
aking words impossible to hear. He walked from the door-
ay to lay down on the grass and let still-aching muscles
lax. The sun had reached the noon sky when he heard the
bin door open, and he rose on one elbow to see Mai-lin
ome out first. She walked down the slope and he called to
er. "Where are you going?" he asked.

"To pick some flowers," she answered.

"Stay in sight," he told her, and she nodded.

He heard Millicent hurrying up behind him, and he rose
face the brilliantly blazing blue eyes.

"I want to talk to you," she began angrily.

"Be my guest," he said.

She drew a deep breath and her full breasts pressed hard
ainst her white blouse. "Mai-lin has this idea in her head
d I can't shake it loose. I want you to talk to her. I want
u to tell her you don't want her to do this," Millicent said.

Fargo let his lips purse in thought. "I can't do that," he
id gravely.

"Of course you can," she said with exasperation.

"No, it wouldn't be right," he said. "I'd be insulting her,"
said, and assumed a concerned look.

"That's the weakest excuse I've ever heard," Millicent
rew back.

"Give me a minute. I'll come up with something better He smiled affably.

"Damn you, Fargo, she's doing this because of an ancien teaching, some outdated code of honor," Millicent said.

"Guess I'll just have to go along with her," Fargo sa helplessly.

"You're impossible. I should've known better. You're ju taking advantage of a chance to enjoy yourself. Haven't yo any sense of decency?" she flung at him.

"Sure I do, but it doesn't tell me to be a damn fool." H grinned.

"You're rotten," she hissed.

"You want to stand in for her?" he suggested.

"No, of course not," Millicent snapped. "Besides, couldn't. I mean, it wouldn't satisfy Mai-lin's code honor."

"That why you're so hot and bothered about this Millicent's eyes shot blue sparks and her hand came up smash across his face. He caught her wrist and spun he away.

"Bastard," she bit out as she spun on her heel and stro back to the cabin. He heard the door slam shut as h stretched out on the slope and watched Mai-lin walk up th hill toward him with her arms full of flowers. She halte beside him, sank down to her knees with a smooth, gracef movement.

"What do you call these flowers?" she asked.

"You've got lavender, wild roses, and the yellow ones a honeysuckle," he said.

She smiled happily. "I must boil them in water. I can u: a kettle I saw in the cabin," she said. She rose and he got his feet with her. "I shall come when the moon rises high she said.

"Millicent is pretty damn mad about it," he said, ar watched her sharply.

Mai-lin's smooth face grew sad. "I know, and I am sorry that. I have never seen her like this. I do not understand she said. "I almost think there is what you call jealousy her anger."

"I think you're pretty damn wise for someone so young." go grinned.

"The Tao says there are two kinds of wisdom, the wisdom t comes from the world and the wisdom that comes from heart," she answered. The almond-shaped eyes held h sadness and a smile. "Tonight," she murmured, and ried up the slope.

argo watched her go for a moment and then slowly wan-ed down the slope and into the trees. He paced along treeline, surveying, measuring, making a half-dozen s back and forth. When he returned to the cabin, he nmaged and found three tin cans and some string. Hur-g back down the slope to one end of the treeline, he set is task and finished as the day began to fade. When he urned to the cabin, he found Millicent waiting inside.

I just want you to know one thing," she began. "I'm not ying in the next cabin while you're indulging yourself and ing advantage of Mai-lin's sense of honor."

You want to go out and let a Kiowa take advantage of , go ahead," Fargo said.

Your actions are sending me out," she pushed at him.

Good try, but no cigar." He grinned.

You'd go ahead with this, knowing I won't stay next r?" She frowned.

I don't take to stupidity. Or jealousy. You're running h both," he said.

You don't have any conscience at all, do you?" she used.

It's there. I don't like to use it when I don't have to. ars it out," he said.

he flung a bitter glance at him and paused in the door-

way. "Anything happens to me, you'll have to live with i
she threatened.

"Guess so," he said as she stormed from the cabin.
heard the door slam in the next cabin as he stretched out
the bunk bed. He didn't turn the lamp on and let darkn
fill the room. When the first pale trickle of moonlight
tered into the room, he rose, closed the door, and lifted t
top bed off the support. He put it one corner of the ro
and stretched out on it as the moonlight grew stronger.
hadn't waited long when he heard the faint knock.

"It's open," he called, and watched the slender, sup
shape come into the room. Mai-lin closed the door behi
her, paused, and let her eyes grow used to the pale li
inside the cabin. She carried a small cup in one hand. S
found him and came at once to kneel down beside him.
swung his long legs over the edge of the bed frame and to
her face in his hands. Her deep eyes met his, her sloe-ey
loveliness entirely composed. "You don't have to do th
you know," he said.

"But I want to, Fargo," she said.

"Because of what you believe. That's a different kind
wanting," he said.

The little smile that touched her lips held a wise slyne
"It is that and it is more," she said softly. "You are beautif
I look at you and feel my body glow. It is the kind of want
you mean. It is also said by the wise men that to give ones
to an exceptional person is a gift returned, and you are a s
cial person, Fargo."

He sighed and drew her to him. Who am I to argue w
Chinese wisdom he muttered silently. Her lips press
gently against his mouth, a sweet, light touch, a hint an
promise. She moved back and began to unbutton his sh
"I can do that," he said.

"No, it is for me," she answered. "A girl of high so

osition is taught many things so when the time comes she
may please the mind, the eye, and the body."

He lay back and let her unbutton his shirt, and when she
gently took it from him, her hands caressed his chest with
smooth, sliding motions. She undid the gun belt and let it
drop to the floor, then began to open his trousers, and he
felt himself responding to her touch. She removed his trousers and then his shorts, and he rose instantly erect and
throbbing. But she took the little cup, dipped one hand in
, and began to massage his body with a soft liquid that both
soothed and stimulated. He smelled the scent of the roses
and honeysuckle in it, backed by the dark scent of the
lavender.

"I boil the flowers and their liquid comes from them. I
mix it with a little honey," she said, sensing his thoughts.
Her hands moved down his chest, across his hard-muscled
abdomen, down into his groin, her touch almost fleeting yet
firm, and when she reached his pulsing, eager organ, he felt
her fingers slide up and down the shaft, a fleeting touch and
then gone, but the excitement spiraled through him. Mai-
lin rose, stood beside him, and with a slow, utterly graceful
movement, pulled the gown over her head to stand naked at
his side.

He gasped at the absolute grace and symmetry of her
slender, supple body. Her high, small breasts were suddenly magnificently beautiful, perfectly curved, perfectly
shaped, tiny little pink points in the exact center of each
perfect circle. His gaze followed the curve of her body to
the very small waist and down to legs, which were so perfectly shaped they seemed longer than they were; slender
hips and long, slender thighs; smooth, unblemished skin; a
tiny little convex tummy, and beneath it, almost no nap at
all, her pubic mound curving outwards in unadorned
splendor.

Mai-lin came to him, pressed her lips to his for another

quick kiss, and then drew away and knelt down beside him, her lips moving down his body, across his chest first, pausing to pull gently at his nipples, her tongue caressing each, then moving down over his abdomen: slow, tantalizing movements, kissing, nibbling, pressing with the faintest touch. He felt as though a sensuous butterfly were moving back and forth across his body as she nibbled down over his belly, her tongue darting out to touch, caress, and move on. He felt her push through the dark tangle and pause at the base of his throbbing shaft, and he was aflame. "Jesus," he gasped out as she began to move her lips up the waiting eager maleness, nibbling motions again and then, as she reached the top, pulling away. "Goddamn," he growled as he reached for her, pulled her up to him, and heard her tiny velvet laugh.

He closed his mouth over one small breast, sucked it in and heard her long cry of delight. "Ah . . . ah . . . aaaaaaah," Mai-lin sighed, and her hands fluttered up and down his back, pressed gently, then harder, came down to clasp his buttocks. He felt the almost napless little mount rub against him, and he drove forward to find her, impale her, but she swung her legs to the side, slipped almost from his grasp, and as he turned, she slid down to press her face against him, nibble again along the pulsating shaft. When she reached the top, she paused for an instant and then enveloped him in the warmth of her lips. She pulled, kissed, caressed, nibbled, sucked, and edged him with tiny touches of her teeth, and he felt himself about to explode when she finally drew away.

He turned, came over her, and this time her slender legs lifted, clasped around his waist. She thrust upward and met his nearly exploding maleness in a moment of unexpected savage intensity, and he felt the tightness of her burst apart as she screamed, a cry of pleasure-pain. He paused but she drew back only to thrust upward at once.

158

The soft, caressing, sweet delicateness vanished into ard, long, thrusting passion, and with each thrust, Mai-lin reamed in ecstasy and cried out words in her own tongue at needed no translation. He couldn't hold back and xploded within her as she cried out, clung to him, held her gs tight around him. "More," she breathed. "More, more, ore." She began to move her hips in slow, undulating otions, and he felt her pressing her wet warmth against m, instantly arousing, inflaming. Mai-lin's almond eyes ere almost closed, but her lips stayed open to kiss his face, ad his tongue, pull him to her.

He felt himself growing, ballooning inside her, and heard er little cry of delight. "Yes, yes, more, more, more," she sped again. The soft undulating motion changed, became ng, slow thrusts that grew harsher. "Ah . . . aaaah . . . aaaah," Mai-lin groaned, and she drew her supple figure ckward, pushed forward, drew her stomach in and thrust forward, each motion a welcome and a demand, and sud-nly he heard her groans grow deeper until they were only allow breaths. He slid slowly back and forth inside her d she met his every thrust, and suddenly he heard her himper. "Fargo . . . oh, oh, Fargo," she breathed, and ith it he felt her legs grow tight around him. Her hands ug into his shoulders and she lifted herself up to cling ainst him. "It is . . . it is," she cried out, and suddenly she as shaking, violent spasms coursing through her, her arm tunnel tightened around him in fierce little spasms. ne whispered cry grew, became a scream of pure ecstasy she clung to him, and he came with her, erupting against e tight spasms, and again she screamed.

She stayed against him, violently shaking, until suddenly er head fell back, her eyes closed, and he felt her body go np as a rag doll. He let her drop to the bed and lay down side her. His gaze took in the loveliness of her, as beauti- spent as aroused. Her eyes opened slowly and a tiny

smile edged her lips. Her arms reached up to encircle h[...]
neck. "A gift returned," she whispered, and cradled his fa[...]
against the small, perfectly formed breasts.

He fell asleep with her until he was wakened by the tou[...]
of a butterfly against his skin. He glanced down to see h[...]
long black hair across his chest as she nibbled her way dow[...]
his body. He reached down, found her shoulders, a[...]
pulled her up to him.

"It is morning," she said. "Let us welcome the day wi[...]
the echoes of the night."

"Why not?" he agreed, and she turned back to move h[...]
lips across his body in a tracery of tiny fiery lines. He w[...]
aflame in moments and the new sun slipped through t[...]
window with her cry of new ecstasy. He lay with her un[...]
she finally rose and stretched the beautifully supple bod[...]
As he watched her, he decided she was like a Chinese va[...]
he'd once seen—graceful, small, perfectly proportioned.

She slipped the pale-blue dress on and came to him.[...]
am glad," she said. "I feel good."

"I feel pretty damn good myself," Fargo said. She l[...]
with a soft kiss and he put on trousers and gun belt a[...]
walked to the door. He spotted Millicent sitting with kne[...]
drawn up halfway down the slope and he wandered down[...]
her. She continued to stare into the lush landscap[...]
"Thought you were leaving," he said.

"I changed my mind," she muttered, turned, a[...]
searched his face. "You're not surprised." She frowned.

"Nope," he said.

"Why not?" She glared. "Been learning Chinese wi[...]
dom?" she added tartly.

"Got my own," he said. "It's called henhouse wisdom.[...]

"What's that mean?" she protested.

"Tell you some other time." He laughed. "Now why do[...]
you make some coffee and I'll rustle up some fruit."

'I want to know what you meant by that," she said as she
. to her feet.

"Some other time," he said again as he wandered down
: hill. When he returned with wild pears and plums,
llicent had the coffee ready to drink. Mai-lin welcomed
n with a big smile and ate hungrily. Millicent picked at
: fruit but managed to finish breakfast, he noted. The
men went to the brook and he sat by the cabin door and
:ened while he scanned the hills below. When they
urned, Millicent left her shirt hanging out loose and the
» buttons undone. The swell of her breasts rose in a full
've over the edge of the last button, and he followed both
ls into the cabin.

'I want to search around," he said. "See what's here."

"There were some boxes. We pushed them under the
nk the other night," Millicent said.

He knelt down and dragged the three boxes into the open
l let out a snort of satisfaction as he examined the largest
the boxes. "Gunpowder," he said. "Might come in real
dy."

The other boxes held smaller amounts of gunpowder, he
v. He pushed the boxes into a corner and sprang to his
t as he picked up the sound of a horse. Pressing himself
inst the open door, he scanned the line of trees halfway
vn the slope. A lone horseman appeared, riding slowly,
: flat-brimmed hat unmistakable. Fargo stepped outside
Joseph came to a halt.

'Damn old fox," Fargo said, and a smile creased the
ind face.

"Figured you do something, Fargo," Joseph said.

'You get to the U.S. marshal?" Fargo asked as Millicent
l Mai-lin stepped out of the cabin.

'He has girls and old man," Joseph said. "But too short of
puties to go after Thorenson. Make no difference, any-
y. Thorenson and his men out to find you and girl. I see

them reach river. Maybe one, two days before they f[i]
tracks."

Fargo nodded. "What else?" he asked.

"Marshal say bring everybody else to him. He take eve[ry]
one to army post at Bear Lake. Everybody safe ther[e]
Joseph said.

"Can you get past Thorenson's men?" Fargo asked.

"If they stay busy here with you," Joseph answere[d]
"They find nobody here, they come after us."

"It's Mai-lin he really wants," Millicent said. "Take h[er]
I'll stay here with Fargo."

"No, you have done enough for me already," Mai-lin s[aid]
to her.

"You'll make better time with two horses. Take the gra[y]
Millicent said to Joseph. "I'll saddle him up." She spun a[nd]
hurried around to the back of the cabin.

"No, it is not right. Millicent has done so much for m[e]
She must come with me," Mai-lin said to Fargo.

"Let her be," Fargo said. "You don't often get to do som[e]
thing for somebody else and yourself at the same time."

"I do not understand." Mai-lin frowned.

"Don't try," he told her.

She reached out, put her hand to his face. "I hoped [for]
another night, Fargo," she murmured.

"It would've been real nice," he agreed as Millic[ent]
rounded the cabin with the gray in tow. She embraced M[ai-]
lin for a long moment and then helped her into the sadd[le]

"One thing more, Fargo," Joseph said, his round f[ace]
grave. "Tarawa searches for you. He knows the man on t[he]
Ovaro wreck his attack on fort. He has made promise to [kill]
you. You watch good, Fargo."

"I will," Fargo said. "Now get moving." He met Mai-li[n's]
soft, dark eyes for a moment more, and then she turned [to]
follow Joseph. He headed across the slope and away fr[om]

162

trees halfway down, and Fargo smiled to himself as he
pped into the cabin.

We just wait now?" Millicent asked.

We arrange a reception for the good trader Thorenson,"
go said. "First, we take the two small cases of the gun-
vder and put them in the other cabin. The big one stays
e." Millicent nodded and helped him carry the cases.
ack them together in that corner," he said.

he followed directions and hurried after him as he
urned to the other cabin. He used a tin cup to take some
he gunpowder from the case, and he drew a line across
cabin floor with it until he reached the rear wall. He
hed enough of the gunpowder through the cracks in the
in logs until the trail ended in a small mound just out-
e. As Millicent watched, he cut a length of lariat, ran it
into the fir trees behind the cabin, and wedged the
er end into the gunpowder at the wall of the cabin. Fin-
ed, he stood up, surveyed the primitive fuse, and
pped back, satisfied.

I'll see that they rush the cabins," he said. "That won't
too hard. They'll figure they have us trapped." He
nced up to see night sweeping down from the mountains
ind them. "Keep your lamp out," he said as he walked to
front of the cabins.

You didn't run a fuse from the powder boxes in your
in," she reminded him.

No need for it. When this one goes, they'll blow," he
wered. "Put your gear on the Ovaro," he said. "Just in
e we have to make a run for it." She nodded and he
ted in the doorway as she carried her saddlebag out. He
ched her return, pause, and look at him as the darkness
sed down over the twin cabins. "Sleep light," he said as
closed the door.

Ie undressed to shorts and stretched out on the bunk
l he'd placed on the floor. He was smiling when the door

163

crashed open. "Goddamn you, Fargo," Millicent shouted
she kicked the door shut. He swung to his feet and met [
as she came toward him. His mouth came down hard on [
lips and she twisted away from him. "No," she said, but
reached out, closed a hand over one full breast. "Oh, Go
she breathed.

"No goddamn second thoughts, not now," he muttered
he lifted her and flung her onto the mattress. He sank do
beside her as the moonlight streamed into the cabin.

"Bastard," she spit at him even as she pulled the blo
open. The twin, full breasts fell out, soft and full with v
pink nipples almost overshadowing very small aureoles.
mouth seized one and she gasped out, her hands pulling
his hair. "Bastard," she cried out again, and he helped [
as she frantically pushed her skirt down. Wide, full hips a
lovely thighs opened for him and closed, and a dense, cu
tangle beckoned. He pushed his hand over it, pressed do
on the soft mound beneath it, and she half-screamed. "N
no, oh, God, oh, God," she cried out as he touched the s
ness of the dark entranceway. She was wet, flowing, wa
ing bursting from her, and he responded to her frenzy
frenzy made of fury and wanting, fear and desire, all
contradictions too long bottled up. No gentle tenderness
Millicent, not now, not this first time, he knew. The fe
had to explode when she exploded. His mouth found [
full breast, drew it in, and he felt the nipple grow er
under his tongue. Her hands struck at him, clawed, str
again even as she gasped in desire.

"Damn you," she whispered, and her thighs fell open
him, her moistness against his leg. He brought
throbbing organ to her, laid it atop the dark tangle, and [
scream vibrated the walls of the cabin. "Oh . . . iiiiiee
. . . oh, my God, be careful, be careful . . . iiiiieeeee."
moved, brought the eager organ to the soft lips, and [
thighs straightened, drew up, fell open. "Ah, ah, Jesus,

, no . . . yes . . . bastard . . . oh, oh, oh, please,"
llicent screamed, and the near-blond hair flew back and
th as her head rolled from side to side. He thrust into
r, swiftly, harshly, and her scream became a guttural
)an, rising to a wild cry. He moved inside her, rode with
e frenzied response that exploded as she furiously
mped, her firm rear bouncing up and down, her heels
g into the bed.

She cursed at him, called names as she asked for more,
d he felt her teeth go into his shoulder, tear away, and her
nds pull his mouth down to her breasts. Millicent's arms
l away suddenly and he saw her eyes grow wide, a kind of
ror sweeping over her. Her lips opened and she gasped
words. "Oh, my God, oh, my God," she breathed, and
e half-rose under him, her torso twisting away from him
her legs drew up against the underside of his thighs.

Her scream rose into the air as her face turned away from
n, and just as suddenly her torso twisted back and she
ried her face against him as her scream drained itself to a
)an. "My God," she whispered into his chest, and fell
ck onto the bed. She lay staring at him, the brilliant blue
es glazed.

He watched expression slowly come back into them. "It
res you when a volcano erupts," he said.

"I guess so," Millicent breathed.

"Specially one that's been bottling itself up for so long,"
commented.

She propped herself onto one elbow, and he let his eyes
ive down the lovely curve of her breast as it dipped
vard him. "You knew it could happen, didn't you?" she
d. "You knew it all the time." She searched his face. "Is
t why you knew I wouldn't leave last night?" she asked,
d he nodded. "What'd you mean by henhouse wisdom?"
e pressed.

"Hen wants a rooster, she doesn't go far from the h[en] house," he said, and grinned.

"You are a bastard," Millicent said, but there was admi[ra]tion in her voice.

"You did me out of a week of fun. You ready to make it [up] to me now?" he asked.

"Yes." She nodded. "Damn you, yes." Her arms came [up] to encircle his neck and she pulled him down against [her] breasts. "Oh, God, Fargo, make it happen again for [me] please."

"Never refuse a lady," he said, and drew one soft-fir[m] full breast into his mouth. He felt her stomach suck in [at] once as she gasped in delight. He caressed her breasts w[ith] his lips, drew tiny circles of flame around the nipples w[ith] his tongue.

Millicent's hips twisted, rose, fell back again. Her ha[nd] reached down, searched, found him, and drew away [at] once, crept forward just as quickly again to encircle [the] throbbing warmth of his erectness. She slipped out fr[om] under him, turning to move down along his hard-musc[led] frame. "Let me. I've never . . . let me," she murmured. [He] sank back and felt her exploring, probing caresses t[hat] were perhaps even more exciting for their eager enjoyme[nt.] "Oh, God, oh, my God," Millicent murmured. "Wond[er]ful, Jesus . . . so wonderful." She suddenly uttered a sh[ort] cry of overwhelming delight and pulled him against [her] breasts, rubbed his vibrancy across her nipples, and cr[ied] out with pleasure at the sensation.

He heard her breath grow quicker, shallower, and [he] pulled her over onto her back, came to her, and drove i[nto] her with hurried ecstasy. She screamed in delight. Her f[ull] soft thighs pressed against his hips as she pushed and pul[led] with him, and once again she began to pump with frenz[ied] motions. He kept pace with her, heard her little cries g[row] sharper, hold in her throat, and suddenly explode as [she]

166

under him. "Aaaaiiiii . . . oh, God, oh, yes, yes . . . ai ai . . . aaaaiiiii," Millicent screamed and gasped as she nbled against him, and her eyes grew wide again with or for a brief instant as she came with him, sucking, ing, contracting, until she fell away to stare at him as if n another place in time and space. He held inside her as watched her slowly return and the wildness leave her s. "Is it always that way, like running out of yourself?" asked.

More for some, less for others," he said. "But that's how ught to be. You're a natural, Millicent."

Millie," she said, and curled herself against him as he ghed. She found a comfortable place in the crook of his and he listened to her fall into a satisfied sleep. A warm d brushed against the cabin and he let himself sleep ide her warmth as the night slowly made its way toward ning. The dawn was still holding back when he heard a nd, and he sat up at once. Millie drew herself alongside and it came again, almost a tinkling sound.

What is it?" she asked, alarm in her voice.

Stones rattling inside tin cans tied onto string along the e of the trees," he said. "I put them there so's we'd know en company came."

Why didn't they rattle when Joseph came?" She vned.

Joseph knows me. He looked for the string and found Fargo grinned. "Get dressed, quick and quiet." He ung from the bed and pulled on clothes as he peered out window. The night was still black and he was glad for t. Millicent, dressed now, came to stand beside him. llow me," he told her as he edged the door open just ugh to slip outside. He closed it again, silently, and ed in a crouch as he made his way through the narrow ce between the two cabins. He halted when he reached rear corner of the cabins and dropped to one knee.

Dawn had begun to send pink fingertips along the sky. "⌐
stay here for now," he said to Millie.

"Where are you going?" she asked quickly.

"Just up front," he said. "They'll try to bargain with
but from where they are they won't be able to see m⌐
They'll think I'm answering them from inside the ca⌐
When the shooting starts, you take the Ovaro and go ⌐
into the firs, plenty deep. Stay there till I come for you⌐

He started to turn and move back along the pass⌐
between the cabins as the sky quickly began to grow li⌐
Her hand caught at his arm. "Be careful," she said. "Yo⌐
a week's fun to collect."

"That'll sure keep my head down," he said, grinn⌐
"Now and later." He hurried off in a low crouch ⌐
dropped to his stomach a few inches back of the front ⌐
of the cabin. The day pushed itself into being and he saw⌐
line of riders move from the trees. He counted ⌐
Thorenson in the center of the line as they started up ⌐
slope.

Thorenson halted halfway up. "Fargo," he called.

"That's my name," Fargo called back.

"Give us the girl, that's all we want," the man said. "⌐
don't have to get yourself killed. Give us the girl and ⌐
go on."

"Go to hell," Fargo shouted back.

He saw the line edge a few feet forward. "Don'⌐
dumb," Thorenson called. "Just give us the China girl.⌐

"You want her, you come take her, you rotten son ⌐
bitch," Fargo called. He raised the big Colt in his h⌐
fired, three fast shots, and saw two of the riders topple⌐

"Take him," he heard Thorenson shout. "Fire." He ⌐
the riders spread out and race forward, rifles rai⌐
pouring lead at the two cabins. They were doing what ⌐
expected they'd do: lay down a furious barrage as they r⌐
forward to cover their approach. He was running ⌐

hrough the passageway as the shots shattered the cabin
indows and thudded into the walls. He disdained most of
he fuse and lit only half of it with a match as he raced for the
hite firs. He reached the trees, paused to glance back.
Most of Thorenson's men had reached the two cabins and
e heard them shouting as they leapt to the ground and
lew the doors open with gunfire. He saw the burning fuse
each the powder at the wall, and he dived headfirst into the
ees. The explosion flung him another ten feet and he
runted in pain as he careened against a tree trunk.

He hit the ground, rolled, shook his head, and pushed
imself onto his elbows in time to see the two cabins sailing
to the air in bits and pieces along with assorted arms, legs,
nd torsos. He got to his feet, ran into the firs, and saw
Millicent beside the Ovaro, her mouth agape. "My God,
ou're all right," she gasped. "Every tree around me
hook."

"Hit the saddle," he said as he swung onto the Ovaro,
eached down and pulled her up behind him. She put both
rms around him as he sent the Ovaro racing forward, out of
he trees and past the place where the two cabins had been.
he slope was littered with debris and bodies, but halfway
own the hill he saw Thorenson pulling himself to his feet,
ne of his men still on the ground holding his hands to his
ead. Fargo pulled the big Sharps from its saddle holster
nd put it to his shoulder as he reined up. "Thorenson," he
alled. "You're out of business."

The man turned, saw him, and pulled a gun from his belt.
argo fired once and Thorenson spun around in a full circle,
is arms stretching out. When he came full around, he had
nly a gaping hole where there had been a chest. He col-
psed to the ground, a silent mound of red-soaked clothing.

Fargo wheeled the Ovaro around, pushed the rifle back
to its holster, and rode north across the slope. He finally
ft the odor of burning gunpowder behind as he headed

down into a green valley of pine and balsam. He halte
beside a stream and Millicent slid from the saddle, her eye
on him as he dismounted.

"*Hao jan chih ch'i*," she said. "You are special. You follo
your own code and make it work."

He shrugged. "Don't know any other way."

"Now what?" she asked.

"We rest some and work our way back. No hurry," h
answered as his eyes scanned the terrain.

"No hurry," she echoed. "I like that part." She came t
lean against him and he held her as his gaze continued t
sweep the hollows and ridges. He let the horse drink
found a spot under a huge balsam to lie down, and Millicen
slept quickly beside him. He didn't wake her till the noo
sun had moved on. She freshened up at the brook and the
rode slowly through the remainder of the day. He stayed i
the trees as much as possible, moving into the open onl
when they had to climb a ridge or cross a hollow. He saw n
one, no signs, no prints, nothing to cause alarm, but he wa
wary all the same.

Millicent picked up the tension as he halted in the dusl
"What is it? What did you see?" she asked.

"Nothing," he muttered. "Too much nothing. No on
rides. They're all staying low."

"Tarawa?" she asked.

"He's sent the word. He wants nothing to distract hin
nothing to interrupt his concentration. When he sees
pinto, he wants it to be my Ovaro," Fargo said grimly.

"He failed in his attack on the fort, yet he still carries th
much weight?" Millicent questioned.

"They honor his need to avenge his defeat. They give th
chance to him," Fargo said. "Even the others, the Shoshor
and the Sioux, will respect that."

"They'll help him find you?"

"No, but they'll give him every chance. They'll stay out of s way," Fargo said.

"A fine line of distinction," Millicent said, sniffing.

"Maybe, but it's their line," Fargo said. "They'll stay by " He laid his sleeping bag out over a bed of nut moss and illicent shed clothes to lay hard against him.

"Any reason why we can't?" she asked.

"None," he said, and felt her hands move down to find m, a tremor of pleasure running through her at the oment of touch. He let her begin, find her rhythm, and en frenzied pleasure overtook her, he used his knowl- ge and strength give her wildness direction. Her scream ultimate gratification echoed through the Wind River ountains to match the cry of the eagle.

She slept the night and woke only when he stirred from r arms with the morning sun. When they'd dressed and ten some jerky he had in his saddlebag, he rode down the mainder of the foothills and his gaze move relentlessly ck and forth over the land. "Nothing," he muttered. "Not en a damn pony print."

"Maybe he's called it off. Maybe he got tired looking," illicent offered.

Fargo shrugged. It was unlikely, but the Kiowa could ve gone off in the wrong direction. "We'll be back at the ver, come morning. He should've showed by now if he as here," Fargo pondered aloud. "He'd know that if I ach the river he'll have no more tracks to follow."

"Maybe he doesn't think you'll try for the river. It's the gical place to head for, and maybe he figures you'll expect m to try to get you before you reach it," Millicent said.

"That's just what I hope he's thought," Fargo said. "I'm nking he'll outsmart himself."

He moved the Ovaro on until a stretch of open land sepa- ted him from the next stand of woods. He examined the rrounding hills for a long time before he moved the Ovaro

forward into a fast trot. He felt the crick in his neck fro
turning back and forth to scan the terrain on all sides whe
he reached the woodland, and he let loose a deep sigh
relief in the shadowed hush of the trees. The wooded lar
held until night began to descend and he reined up whe
another stretch of open land lay before him, a small vall
that dipped to another line of heavy timber.

"The river's just past the far stand of trees," he said. "B
we camp here for the night. If we have to run for it dow
that valley, I want the Ovaro rested overnight." He d
mounted and helped Millicent down. They finished off t
jerky, and the warm night made the bedroll almost unne
essary. He lay down atop it and Millicent found his li
almost at once. He let his tongue play with her for a whi
before drawing away. "We sleep tonight, nothing else,"
told her.

"Why?" She frowned.

"I don't think you can do it without screaming," he sai

"You're right," she agreed, and put her head onto
chest. "You've got to make it up to me tomorrow."

"It's a deal," he said, and she curled up beside him a
slept in minutes. He lay awake listening to the night soun
and heard only the creatures of the dark. But then if t
Kiowa were near, he wouldn't hear them, Fargo remind
himself grimly. He half-turned and closed his eyes, the C
only inches from his hand.

It was daylight before Millicent stirred, and he snapp
awake instantly. She rolled on her back, her breasts pushi
upward deliciously. She pulled his face down into the swe
softness between their curving loveliness and he broug
his hands down to grasp each eager breast. He heard t
rush of air only a split second before the lance embedd
itself a fraction of an inch from the side of his head, the lo
pole quivering against his face. Millicent screamed
terror. Fargo stayed motionless for a long moment and ke

er from moving with the weight of his body. The Colt lay
bove her head where his hand had rested as he slept, too
r away to reach now. He turned his head slowly to see the
iowa chief on a pony, his piercing, fierce eyes riveted on
im.

Fargo took in the four braves on their ponies nearby,
ach with bowstring drawn, an arrow trained on him. He
ushed himself to his feet slowly and the Kiowa chief moved
is pony a step forward, close enough for him to yank the
nce back. He raised and held it out, the stone point push-
g at the man who had destroyed his plans.

Fargo stepped back, aware he was clad only in shorts.
arawa moved forward, the lance point only inches from
argo's chest. He backed again and found himself in the
pen land. Tarawa pushed the lance at him again and once
ore Fargo backed away. He glanced at Millicent. She was
her feet, her eyes filled with terror. One of the braves
d moved his pony to stand between her and the Ovaro.
argo half-circled, brought his eyes back to Tarawa. The
ur braves didn't concern him. They wouldn't interfere.
his was Tarawa's revenge, and he alone could take it. The
dian raised the lance and Fargo saw him change his grip
the weapon. He saw the Kiowa dig heels into his pony's
de and the horse charged. Fargo twisted as he dived to
e side and felt the lance graze his back.

He rolled and regained his feet, but the short-legged
ny had turned and Tarawa raced at him again, jabbing
ith the lance as Fargo leapt aside. The wicked point
ashed past him, but the Indian flipped the other end of the
ng pole sideways. Fargo saw it come at him and tried to
ick, but the pole slammed into his forehead. He felt him-
lf go backward and down, flashing lights going off in his
ead. Instinct made him roll, and the lance thudded into
e spot where he had been a split second before. He rolled
gain and the flashing lights disappeared. He leapt to his

feet just in time to see the Kiowa charging at him with th[e] lance upraised. Tarawa flung the weapon and Farg[o] dropped, twisted, and winced in pain as the lance glance[d] off his shoulder. He whirled and tried to seize the weapo[n] but the pony thundered into him and he had to jump awa[y.] Tarawa scooped up the lance as he went past, wheeled h[is] pony around, and charged again. Fargo held his ground [as] long as he dared before leaping sideways. But the Kiow[a] chief had anticipated his move and swerved the pony. Th[e] horse's chest slammed into him, nearly wrenching his bone[s] from their sockets.

He hit the ground and painfully got to his feet agai[n,] grimly circling as the Indian moved his pony to matc[h] Fargo's maneuvers. It was but a matter of time, Farg[o] knew, before one of the Kiowa's lunges hit home. Fatigu[e] would take its toll on his timing. He had only one chanc[e] getting the Kiowa off his pony. Fargo feinted to one side [as] he saw Tarawa start toward him again; the Indian swerve[d] the pony at once. He feinted again, to the other side th[is] time, and once again the Indian instantly swerved the pon[y.]

Fargo tensed his powerful leg and thigh muscles [as] Tarawa charged, and he saw the Indian's black ey[es] watching his feet to see which way he was going to dive. H[e] started to go left, and Tarawa swerved the pony at once [to] counter his move. Fargo continued to go to his left an[d] Tarawa charged, certain he had his quarry this time. H[e] raised the lance to strike when Fargo spun and leapt in[to] the pony instead of away from it. He crashed into the side [of] the horse, gritted his teeth against the pain of it, an[d] clamped one powerful arm around the Indian's leg. H[e] yanked and the Kiowa came off the back of his pony as th[e] steed raced on. Tarawa landed on his back but kept hold [of] the lance. Fargo dropped with both knees onto the Kiowa['s] belly and heard the man grunt in pain. He brought [a] smashing pile driver right down onto the Indian's jaw, an[d]

174

arawa's head swiveled to one side. Fargo saw the lance fall
om his hand and he dived for the weapon and caught it just
s it hit the ground.

He fell with it, whirled, and started to bring it around,
ut saw that the Kiowa had risen to one knee, a long-
andled hunting knife in one hand. Tarawa dived at him
nd Fargo had no time to bring the lance around to use it
roperly, but he swung the pole upward and jammed it
nder the Indian's jaw. Tarawa's head snapped back and he
ll sideways. Fargo smashed the pole down against the
iowa's throat and heard the man's gargled gasp for breath.
e lifted the pole with both hands, crashed it down on the
ndian's throat again as Tarawa tried to rise; the man's lar-
nx ruptured, the front of his neck crushed almost in half. A
out of blood erupted from the Indian's hanging jaw and
argo stood up, the lance still in his hand.

His breath rasped in his throat as his eyes swept over the
ur braves sitting their ponies. Silently they turned away
d walked their ponies slowly into the forest. It was over.
or now. Perhaps there would be another time, another
ace. The struggle would be joined again then. But this
as over. Defeats, like victories, were taken separately, one
y one. The braves vanished into the woods and Fargo let
e lance fall from his hands as Millicent raced toward him.

She reached him, pressed herself to him, the brilliant
lue eyes still full of terror. "My God, I thought you were
nished," she murmured.

He followed her eyes as she looked down at the broken
ody of Tarawa . . . Thunder Chief. She studied Fargo as
e continued to stare at the Kiowa. "What are you think-
g?" she asked.

"He sure was a sore loser," Fargo commented.

Millicent shook her head as she led him back to the trees.
Let's get away from here," she said as she pulled on
othes. He dressed and helped her up into the saddle. He

let the horse slowly pick his way across the little valley an
the sun warmed the land. "We heading back now?" sh
asked.

"In time," he said. "I still have most of a week to collect.

"I thought it was two weeks," Millicent said.

"Come to think of it, it *was* two weeks," Fargo agreed.

"Might have been three," she said, and he felt th
warmth of her hands press into his thighs.

"Three," he agreed again, and headed the Ovaro toward
hollow of soft pine needles that seemed to wait patiently.

LOOKING FORWARD!

**The following is the opening section
from the next novel in the exciting
Trailsman series from Signet:**

**The Trailsman #36
THE BADGE**

*1861. Deep in Crow country,
where moonshine and blood
set off the drums of war.*

e Fargo sat quietly beside Marshal Wolf Caulder on the
anda of Pierce's only hotel. The two men had tipped
ir chairs back against the wall and were resting with their
les crossed on the hotel's porch railing. Across the street
atted the Wells Fargo express office. A gold mining
m town high in the snow-tipped peaks of Idaho, Pierce's
rket Street was nearly empty as the pitiless, mid-
mer sun poured down on the raw buildings.

big man, over six feet tall, Fargo's thick head of raven-
ck hair reached to his massive, powerful shoulders. He
s dressed in buckskins and a tan wide-brimmed hat,
ich he had tipped forward over his forehead to shield his
s from the sun's glare. Reaching to the floor of the
anda, Fargo lifted a fifth of whiskey to his mouth and
ed on it. Beside him, Wolf Caulder lit a cigarette.

At the moment the two men were discussing the prep[ ]terous dime novels of Erasmus Beadle, of which more t[ ]a dozen were available in the hotel lobby.

"Hard to think anyone would believe that cra[ ]remarked Caulder.

The marshal wore a black, flat-crowned Stetson, a cl[ ]white cotton shirt under his vest, and faded jeans tuc[ ]into scuffed half boots. He was a tall, lean man wit[ ]crooked tilt to his wide shoulders and a black eye patch [ ]covered his right eye. A long, puckered scar ran back fr[ ]his right eye socket to his ear, imparting to that side of [ ]face a crushed, bent look.

"What did you think of Grizzly Bill, that dude who [ ]supposed to 've killed a grizzly with a kitchen knife?" Fa[ ]asked, his hawklike eyes snapping with amusement.

"A real hero, he was—and don't forget that was just a[ ]he wiped out a tribe of Sioux with a single six-shooter."

"And of course he never had to reload it."

Caulder chuckled. "Just put it between covers, I gu[ ]That's all it takes to make some people believe just ab[ ]anything."

"Especially Eastern dudes."

"Trouble is, some of them dudes come West to try th[ ]hand at killin' redskins and buffalo."

Fargo shook his head in mild wonderment at the fool[ ]ness of some mortals and watched idly as four men finish[ ]crossing the street and mounted the porch steps lead[ ]into the Wells Fargo express office. A moment later, [ ]glanced up the street and saw a dust-laden rider lead[ ]four saddled mounts down Market Street.

"Now, why would that jasper be leading four sadd[ ]horses into town, do you think?" Fargo asked softly.

Caulder did not answer. But it was obvious he [ ]

loring the same possibility as Fargo. Frowning, Caulder hed his chair gently forward, the wooden legs coming vn without a sound onto the porch. He flicked his ciga- e into the baked dust of Market Street and stood up. go pushed his chair forward also, but he remained sit- ; in it as the two of them watched the approaching rider. • horseman appeared to be leading those four horses ectly toward the express office.

I see what you mean," Caulder said softly to Fargo. aybe you better stay here and keep your ass down."

Caulder removed the marshal's badge from his vest and pped it into his pocket. Fargo understood the move at e. Caulder wanted to get across the street and into that ress office without alerting the rider to the fact that he : a law officer. Snugging his hat down more firmly, lder descended the veranda steps and started across the et. For a moment Fargo watched Caulder go. Then he to his feet and left the veranda to follow him.

Gaining the wooden sidewalk in front of Seth Mabry's bershop, Fargo kept behind Caulder as the marshal con- ed on toward the express office. A covey of snaggle- thed whores swept out of Luke's Saloon and began ;ling when they saw Fargo approaching. Fargo solemnly ched the brim of his hat to the soiled doves as he contin- to follow Caulder.

The horseman was still leading the four saddled mounts vn the street toward the express office. By now he was y a few stores down from the express office. Assuming se four men who had just entered the express office were ding it up, Fargo knew that the marshal was anxious to ar the four before they charged out with guns blazing. In ensuing gunfire, innocent townspeople could easily get down.

Excerpt from THE BADGE

Fargo hung back, his right hand resting on his gun-butt
Caulder mounted the steps and entered the express offi
For long minutes nothing happened. Fargo was beginn
to relax, almost convinced that their fears had been grou
less, the product of a lazy afternoon after having read
many of Beadle's dime novels.

The sudden crash of gunfire told him differently.

Guns blazing, four outlaws broke from the office a
bolted down the steps to their mounts, bulky saddleb
slung over their shoulders. Pulling up, Fargo drew his C
and got off a quick shot, catching the brim of an outlaw's
and snapping it off his head. The five outlaws turned th
guns on Fargo. The fire was heavy enough and one bu
caught Fargo high on the left shoulder, slamming h
backward.

He scrambled into the cover of a nearby doorway. G
blazing, the outlaws mounted up and galloped out of tov
Ignoring his shoulder wound, Fargo flung a couple of fu
shots after them, then dashed up the stairs and into
express office. Wolf Caulder was lying in a pool of his c
blood, the distraught express clerk bending over h
When Fargo leaned close, he saw that Caulder was
shot. It was not a pretty sight.

"Sonofabitch," Caulder whispered to Fargo. "That
Johnny Ringo! An old . . . sidekick."

"And he shot you?"

Caulder nodded, grinning crookedly.

"I think I recognized one of those men," Fargo t
Caulder. "Who were the others?"

". . . don't know."

By this time miners and townsmen had crowded into
tiny office, those behind jostling the men in front as t
tried for a better view of the wounded marshal. Fa

ked up to see the doctor pushing his way through their
ks, using his black bag as a kind of battering ram. Waving
go aside, he bent swiftly to examine Caulder's wound.
n he looked up at the four closest men and told them to
g Caulder over to the saloon. He would have to operate
one of the gaming tables.

Caulder was lifted and carried none too gently out of the
ress office. Fargo followed at a distance, his head
ling, a deadly fatigue falling over his limbs. His shoulder
and was causing him to lose considerable blood, and he
w he should get it tended to as soon as possible. But all
could think of at the moment was taking after Johnny
go—and the stocky outlaw that rode with him.

here were just two more for Skye Fargo to find—and
outlaw he had spotted with Ringo could be one of them.

ater that night Fargo sat a lonely vigil beside the long,
nt figure of Wolf Caulder as he lay unconscious on his
. Caulder did not look good. His color had faded com-
ely. The eye patch had been taken off by the doctor and
 one had bothered to replace it.

s Fargo gazed into the awful, puckered hole where the
shal's eye should have sat, he wondered how the man
ld have sustained such a terrible wound. Not that it mat-
ed any longer. Though the doctor had pushed what was
of Caulder's intestines back into his abdomen and sewn
up, he held little hope for the marshal's survival. He
Fargo that Caulder would be lucky to make it through
night.

fter he took care of Caulder, the doctor had repaired
go's shoulder. The bullet had torn up considerable
scle and nipped an artery. The result was a loss of blood
had left Fargo as weak as a kitten.

Caulder stirred. "Water," he said, his voice barely ab
a whisper.

Fargo filled a glass from a pitcher sitting on the n
table and lifted Caulder's head so he could drink from
glass. Caulder gulped the water gratefully, then coug
most of it back up.

Fargo put the glass back on the table and leaned cl
"Caulder, tell me what happened in that office."

"I walked in and saw Ringo," Caulder whispered so
"I was surprised. It really stopped me. I didn't keep my
on them. I let it drop. Ringo smiled. He seemed glad to
me."

"Then he gut shot you."

"He turned bad, Fargo. Real bad. He's finished me, l
like."

"Hell, Caulder. You ain't dead yet. The doc got the bu
out and he's sewed you up good and proper."

"You know better than that, Fargo. No bullshit, okay

"Okay, Wolf. No bullshit. You got any idea where
Ringo jasper might be headin'?"

"For the past week I been hearin' things . . . there
town in the mountains south of here."

Fargo leaned closer. "Where?"

"Big Rock . . . Lost River Range."

Fargo sat back, frowning. He knew the Lost River co
try. And he had heard of Big Rock.

"Fargo," Caulder whispered hoarsely. A cold sweat
broken out on Caulder's forehead. "Get Ringo—and
rest of them bastards for me, will you?"

Fargo did not hesitate. "I'll do what I can, Caul
That's a promise."

"Take my badge, Fargo. It's in my pocket."

Fargo remembered seeing Caulder pocket his ba

re leaving the veranda. He reached into the man's
et and withdrew the badge.

got it, Caulder."

'm deputizin' you, Fargo. That'll make it all nice and
."

ure, Caulder. But I would have gone after them any-
I'm thinking."

Iell, I knew that," Caulder said, a faint smile creasing
avaged face. Then he closed his eyes. A moment later,
oroken visage seemed to cave in slightly and his long
stretched out. Fargo took a deep breath, then stood
nd looked for a moment down at the man who had low-
his gun at sight of an old friend. And was now a dead
as a result.

rgo pinned on the badge and left the room.

week later Skye Fargo rode slowly into Big Rock astride
andsome Ovaro pinto. His shoulder wound had forced
to spend longer than he wished in Pierce, and at the
ent the wound was forcing him to let his pinto pick his
gait. As he rode, he kept the brim of his hat low enough
ield his eyes from the sun's glare. Ahead of him he saw
athered huddle of buildings crouched in amidst the
ring peaks of the Lost River Range.

plank bridge carried him across the creek into the
. For a while he rode beside empty single-story frame
es, their curtainless windows coated with dust. Soon he
to the row of false-front buildings on both sides of the
t that made up the town's business district. Another
cut south out of the foothills to form an intersection
d of him. On the four corners sat a hotel, a general
, and two large saloons. Across from the hotel, Fargo
the livery stable, and headed for it.

Excerpt from THE BADGE

Easing his pinto to a halt in front of the livery, Fargo
mounted carefully. An old man materialized out of the
ble's gloom, his cheek swollen with tobacco.

"Second stall back," he told Fargo, loosing a black d
to the ground beside him.

Fargo gave the pinto a small drink at the street tr
first, then led him into the stall, where he removed the
dle and the rest of his gear. Leaving the stable, he lu
his saddle and the rest of his gear across the street t
hotel. There was a room with tubs on the first floor in
After he had taken advantage of this luxury, he ate i
hotel's cramped dining room, then drifted through
lobby into the hotel's elaborate saloon.

Taking a seat at a table in the far corner, he sipp
beer and kept his eye on the flipping batwings. They
seldom still. From the look of the saloon's customers, i
obvious that most of the men were on the dodge—w
was one very good reason why Fargo had decided to
his badge in his pocket. The saloon was noisy enough
there was no lack of poker tables or women.

He kept his eyes open, hoping to catch sight of Rin
any of his gang. He was pretty sure he would know R
when he saw him and Fargo was not too discouraged v
after more than two hours, neither Ringo or any of his
members showed up. He would just have to be patie
Ringo's gang wanted a town to celebrate a heist, this w
And if he had been here and gone, Fargo would soon
that out easily enough.

Six percentage girls worked the place, all of them
ously shipped up from Mexico, judging from their
complexions, their dark, sorrowful eyes and long black
hanging past their shoulders. The hotel saloon's owner
too cheap to provide the girls with any fancy, span

resses, but what they wore was low enough in front and igh enough down above the ankles to make up for that ack.

The girls seemed reasonably content with their lot, xcept for one of them, who kept strictly to business, which or her appeared to be waiting on the customers at their ables. Nevertheless, taller than the other girls, with more heat on her bones, she seemed an irresistible attraction to he older, more grizzled patrons. As the evening wore on nd she found herself more and more manhandled, the roud angry light in her eyes flared more openly.

At last, unable to witness the cuffing and casual brutality he girl was being forced to endure, he paid his tab and eturned to the hotel lobby. His long ride that day had tired im considerably, and in addition his shoulder was beginning to ache like a sore tooth. He was anxious to get up to is room so he could tend to it.

He asked the desk clerk for his room key. As the clerk eached for it, Fargo heard a sharp scuffle behind him. He urned. The tall bar girl was being hauled roughly past the esk by two older men. Their yellow teeth gleamed wolf-hly through their tobacco-stained beards. A small fat han—the hotel owner—rushed out of his office behind the esk and tried to talk the two men out of taking the girl pstairs.

But the two men would have none of it.

They were obviously miners. Their boots were heavy vith mud. Their faces and hands were almost black from veeks of pawing in the bowels of the earth. They stank. The ne closest to Fargo was the tallest—a lean, raw-faced man vith sick, furtive eyes.

"Now lookee here, Pablo," he was telling the hotel wner, "Sam and me, we been steady customers this past

year and we always pay up. We know what you're doin'
You're saving up this here Mex for yerself."

"Slim, that ees not true!" the hotel owner cried.

"Never mind that!" Slim replied. "We'll pay you double
tonight. And all of it in gold dust. So leave us be!"

"No!" Pablo said. "You go back in the saloon. I'll send
Dolores to your table. She'll be down soon. Juanita, here
she no want to go upstairs with you two."

"Now, what the hell difference does that make?"

Sam spoke up then. He was a bit unsteady on his feet a
he held the girl's wrist in a viselike grip. "We don't wan
Dolores. It's like screwin' a rain barrel. This here Juanit
suits us fine." Sam grinned at Juanita. " 'Bout time she g
broke in real good and proper."

Slim reached over and grabbed a fistful of Juanita's bu
tocks and squeezed. The girl made a tiny cry. The two me
burst into laughter. The smaller one hauled the girl towar
the stairs, Slim following. Fargo saw that Pablo wa
wavering. The man was obviously unwilling to go agains
the wishes of the two men. On the other hand, he seeme
to care greatly for Juanita and did not want these men t
have her.

Fargo thrust his room key into his pocket, then caugl
the girl's eye—and winked. It was not a playful wink, b
one designed to alert the girl to his intentions. Then h
moved ahead of the two men and positioned himself befor
them at the foot of the stairs.

"Hey, Juanita!" he cried, pulling the girl out of the sta
tled Slim's grasp and into his own arms. "I just go in. I tol
you I'd be here tonight. How come you're with these two'

"Hey!" protested Sam. "Who're you?"

"Hold it right there, mister," Slim said. "She's with us

Ignoring Slim, Fargo tucked his arm around Juanita

aist and leaned close. Into her ears he whispered, "*Play
ong! My name's Skye Fargo!*"

Juanita smiled brilliantly. "Skye!" she cried. "Where
ve you been. I have wait so long for you!"

Patting Juanita on the ass, he sent her up the stairs ahead
him. But the two miners were not deceived. They knew
hat Fargo was doing, and they were furious at his
tervention.

Reaching out, Slim grabbed Fargo's right arm and spun
m about. "You ain't foolin' me, you sonofabitch! I ain't
nna let you—"

That was all he got out. Fargo backhanded Slim across the
eek. The man went reeling back against the wall. Sam
ok a step back and clawed for his gun. But Fargo's own six-
n was out well ahead of the half-soused miner. Before
m could bring up his weapon, Fargo brought the barrel of
s Colt down hard on the smaller man's wrist. The six-gun
attered to the floor.

"*Señor!*"

It was the girl. Fargo whirled. Slim was charging him.
olstering his Colt, Fargo ducked aside and caught the man
he reeled past him. With both hands Fargo propelled the
an, head first, into the wall. Slim shook himself groggily,
en turned and rushed back at Fargo. Fargo waited, then
ove his fist into the man's face, crunching into his nose.
im's head snapped back, a heavy freshet of blood stream-
g from one nostril. Fargo drove in closer and caught Slim
out his head and shoulders in a furious, sledging flurry
at drove Slim out of the lobby and into the saloon.

As Slim disappeared through the doorway and crashed
t of sight to the floor of the saloon, an immediate silence
ll over the saloon. Fargo waited for Slim to pick himself up
d reappear in the doorway. He did not. Fargo turned

back to the other miner. Sam had sunk to the floor, holdi
onto his swollen wrist. His Colt was lying at his feet, but
made no effort to reach for it.

Fargo turned to the girl. "My room is at the head of t
stairs," he told her.

She turned and hurried up the flight ahead of him. Wit
out looking back at the miner or the hotel owner, Fargo f
lowed the girl up the stairs and into his room.

Exciting Westerns by Jon Sharpe from SIGNET

(0451)

THE TRAILSMAN #1: SEVEN WAGONS WEST	(127293—$2.50)*
THE TRAILSMAN #2: THE HANGING TRAIL	(110536—$2.25)
THE TRAILSMAN #3: MOUNTAIN MAN KILL	(121007—$2.50)*
THE TRAILSMAN #4: THE SUNDOWN SEARCHERS	(122003—$2.50)*
THE TRAILSMAN #5: THE RIVER RAIDERS	(127188—$2.50)*
THE TRAILSMAN #6: DAKOTA WILD	(119886—$2.50)*
THE TRAILSMAN #7: WOLF COUNTRY	(123697—$2.50)
THE TRAILSMAN #8: SIX-GUN DRIVE	(121724—$2.50)*
THE TRAILSMAN #9: DEAD MAN'S SADDLE	(126629—$2.50)*
THE TRAILSMAN #10: SLAVE HUNTER	(114655—$2.25)
THE TRAILSMAN #11: MONTANA MAIDEN	(116321—$2.25)
THE TRAILSMAN #12: CONDOR PASS	(118375—$2.50)*
THE TRAILSMAN #13: BLOOD CHASE	(119274—$2.50)*
THE TRAILSMAN #14: ARROWHEAD TERRITORY	(120809—$2.50)*
THE TRAILSMAN #15: THE STALKING HORSE	(121430—$2.50)*
THE TRAILSMAN #16: SAVAGE SHOWDOWN	(122496—$2.50)*
THE TRAILSMAN #17: RIDE THE WILD SHADOW	(122801—$2.50)*
THE TRAILSMAN #18: CRY THE CHEYENNE	(123433—$2.50)*

*Price is $2.95 in Canada

Buy them at your local bookstore or use this convenient coupon for ordering.

NEW AMERICAN LIBRARY,
P.O. Box 999, Bergenfield, New Jersey 07621

Please send me the books I have checked above. I am enclosing $_____ (please add $1.00 to this order to cover postage and handling). Send check or money order—no cash or C.O.D.'s. Prices and numbers are subject to change without notice.

Name_____

Address_____

City_____ State_____ Zip Code_____

Allow 4-6 weeks for delivery.
This offer is subject to withdrawal without notice.

SIGNET Westerns You'll Enjoy by Leo P. Kelley

(04

☐ CIMARRON #1: CIMARRON AND THE HANGING JUDGE (120582—$2.5
☐ CIMARRON #2: CIMARRON RIDES THE OUTLAW TRAIL (120590—$2.5
☐ CIMARRON #3: CIMARRON AND THE BORDER BANDITS
(122518—$2.5
☐ CIMARRON #4: CIMARRON IN THE CHEROKEE STRIP (123441—$2.5
☐ CIMARRON #5: CIMARRON AND THE ELK SOLDIERS (124898—$2.5
☐ CIMARRON #6: CIMARRON AND THE BOUNTY HUNTERS
(125703—$2.5
☐ CIMARRON #7: CIMARRON AND THE HIGH RIDER (126866—$2.5
☐ CIMARRON #8: CIMARRON IN NO MAN'S LAND (128230—$2.5
☐ CIMARRON #9: CIMARRON AND THE VIGILANTES (129180—$2.5
☐ CIMARRON #10: CIMARRON AND THE MEDICINE WOLVES
(130618—$2.5
☐ CIMARRON #11: CIMARRON ON HELL'S HIGHWAY (131657—$2.5

*Price is $2.95 in Canada

**Buy them at your local
bookstore or use coupon
on next page for ordering.**

)

ld Westerns by Warren T. Longtree

e is $2.95 in Canada

JOIN THE *TRAILSMAN* READERS' PANEL

Help us bring you more of the books you like by fill
out this survey and mailing it in today.

1. Book Title: _____

   Book #: _____

2. Using the scale below, how would you rate this book
   the following features? Please write in one rating from 0
   for each feature in the spaces provided.

POOR		NOT SO GOOD			O.K.			GOOD		EXCEL LENT
0	1	2	3	4	5	6	7	8	9	1

RATI

Overall opinion of book .... _____
Plot/Story .... _____
Setting/Location .... _____
Writing Style .... _____
Character Development .... _____
Conclusion/Ending .... _____
Scene on Front Cover .... _____

3. About how many western books do you buy for yours
   each month? _____

4. How would you classify yourself as a reader of westerns
   I am a ( ) light ( ) medium ( ) heavy reade

5. What is your education?
   ( ) High School (or less) ( ) 4 yrs. college
   ( ) 2 yrs. college ( ) Post Graduate

6. Age _____ 7. Sex: ( ) Male ( ) Female

Please Print Name_____

Address_____

City _____ State _____ Zip _____

Phone # ( ) _____

Thank you. Please send to New American Library, Resea
Dept., 1633 Broadway, New York, NY 10019.